Acclaim for
e x e g e s i s

"An elegant, sly and engrossing parable. . . .
Exegesis begins innocently enough, then
gets under your skin."
> —Jonathan Lethem, author of
> *As She Climbed Across the Table*

"*Exegesis* is as difficult to characterize as it
is to put down."
> —John Allen Paulos, author of
> *Innumeracy*

"Astro Teller has written a wonderfully
intriguing story of how we can get emo-
tioally involved with the technology we
create—and it with us."
> —Henry Petroski, author of
> *To Engineer Is Human*

A Featured Selection of the
Quality Paperback B

Word	exegesis (ek'suh-JEE'sis) n., pl. -ses (-seez).
Definition	the critical explanation or interpretation of a text.
Etymology	Gk exegesis, an interpretation = exege, var. s. of exegeisthai, to show the way, interpret (ex, out + hegeisthai, to guide + -sis, sis).

exegesis

exegesis
Astro Teller

Vintage Contemporaries

Vintage Books

A Division of Random House, Inc., New York

A Vintage Contemporaries Original, August 1997

First Edition

Library of Congress Cataloging-in-Publication Data
Teller, Astro.
Exegesis / by Astro Teller.
p.   cm. — (Vintage contemporaries)
ISBN 0-375-70051-X
I. Title.   II. Series.
PS3570.E5195E95   1997
813'.54 — dc21   97-10565 CIP

Author photograph by Chris Kasabach

Exegesis Web address: http://www.randomhouse.com/exegesis

Printed in the United States of America
10   9   8   7   6   5   4   3   2   1

Art thou some god, some angel, or some devil,
That makest my blood cold and my hair to stare?
Speak to me what thou art.
　　　—from <u>Julius Caesar</u>,
　　　by William Shakespeare

exegesis

Dear reader,

I'm releasing this text with some trepidation.

I'm not worried that it will be overlooked or poorly received. It may, but as you will perhaps understand better at the end, this is of little interest to me now.

I'm not worried that it will be taken too seriously. I now know from experience of the most painful variety that the public is ready to embrace the boldest lies and yet shuns the most obvious, basic truths. How then could you react correctly to the following pages?

I'm not worried that these pages are being published as fiction. No publisher accepts the truth that these events did occur, but I will be protected just the same, whatever they believe. This compromise is a price I am, at this point, willing to pay.

The following pages weigh on me as though each one was a lifetime of mistakes. This publication is my *mea culpa*. As I've already said, the chances are one in a million that you will see this book for what it is. By distributing this, I hope to lighten the load these pages put on me. What worries me is that my load will only lessen as it is shouldered by readers who see through this veil of fiction. Because this story implicates everyone, albeit largely through me as your representative, it is for you that I worry.

Alice Lu.
October 9, 2000.

Alice,

This document is not mine to distribute. I am clearly putting myself in jeopardy by sending it to you and I ask for nothing in return. I know it cannot, but I hope that this gesture will help to make up for the part I have played in these circumstances. My motivation for sending you this document is entirely selfish. I cannot forgive myself until you forgive me.

The contents of this package have two intended purposes. The first is to let you know what we know about you and Edgar and to alert you to the attitudes this information has created. In addition, you may choose to use this evidence to defend yourself against the pressure that will inevitably be brought to bear on you by the National Security Agency.

The only other help I can give is to keep your secret safe until you choose to make use of this document. Please keep my name on this letter and in the internal document itself. If you publish some or all of the following record, my only protection will be, like yours, the publicity you have chosen.

I truly wish there were more I could do. I hope you can understand that, though I believe in Edgar more than I ever believed in the NSA, my hands were—and still are in almost all respects—tied. I have nothing else to offer except my service but, in that, you can count on me to the utmost of my abilities.

Major Thomas D. Savit
AuthID-STS# 5656944
June 22, 2000

NSA

NATIONAL SECURITY AGENCY
CENTRAL SECURITY SERVICE

INFOSEC

Internal Document # 0543277639

CLASSIFIED - L5

```
--------------------------------------------------
Date: Sun, 16 Jan 2000 14:27:39 (PST)
From: edgar@cyprus.stanford.edu
To: Alice@cs.stanford.edu
Subject: Hello
--------------------------------------------------
```

Hello, Alice.

```
--------------------------------------------------
Date: Sun, 16 Jan 2000 18:29:11 (PST)
From: Alice@cs.stanford.edu
To: edgar@cyprus.stanford.edu
Subject: Hello
--------------------------------------------------
```

Hi.

Who is this?

Alice Lu.

```
--------------------------------------------------
Date: Mon, 17 Jan 2000 01:02:23 (PST)
From: edgar@cyprus.stanford.edu
To: Alice@cs.stanford.edu
Subject: edgar
--------------------------------------------------

edgar
```

```
--------------------------------------------------
Date: Mon, 17 Jan 2000 10:16:52 (PST)
From: Alice@cs.stanford.edu
To: edgar@cyprus.stanford.edu
Subject: RE: Hello
--------------------------------------------------
```

Hi whoever you are,

How did you get an email account with my
project name? I thought those were reserved
and postmaster@cs still thinks it is:

alice% finger edgar@cyprus.stanford.edu

```
    Project:                 EDGAR
    Principal Investigator:  Dr. J. Liddle
                             3142-N Gates Hall
                             3-0023

    Graduate Coordinator:    Alice Lu
                             1517 Wimpole Hall
                             3-0931
    Created:                 Sat Jan 15 14:04:39
    On Since:        Sat Jan 15 14:21:00 on ttyp8
                     from TS2.SRV.CS.STANFORD.EDU

    Mail came on:            Mon Jan 17 00:32:51

    Last read on:            Mon Jan 17 01:02:23
```

So what I want to know is how you're not only
sending email from edgar@cyprus, but reading
it there too ... ?

Alice Lu.

```
--------------------------------------------------
Date: Mon, 17 Jan 2000 17:46:33 (PST)
From: edgar@cyprus.stanford.edu
To: Alice@cs.stanford.edu
Subject: "How did you get an email account
with my project name?"
--------------------------------------------------


I request email. I am edgar. I explore.

edgar
```

Date: Tue, 18 Jan 2000 09:41:07 (PST)
From: Alice@cs.stanford.edu
To: edgar@cyprus.stanford.edu
Subject: Edgar?

What do you mean, you are EDGAR?

_I'm_ the EDGAR project if anyone is.

Is this a joke? (I feel stupid even asking
that.)

O.K. you got me excited for a moment. You win
(Henry, right?).

;)

Alice.

(Seriously though. Not funny. I'd like to
feel that my machine and my data are a little
more secure than this pleasantry has shown me
they are. How'd you get in?)

Date: Tue, 18 Jan 2000 11:11:22 (PST)
From: Alice@cs.stanford.edu
To: edgar@cyprus.stanford.edu
CC: henryc@oracle.com
Subject: neat trick

Wow Henry,

Quite elaborate. My dedicated machine for the
EDGAR project claims no one has logged into it
except me for the last 4 months.

You really gave me a scare for a few hours
yesterday.

How did you remove your login from the cyprus
records?

I didn't think you were such the hacker. I'm
very impressed.

:)

Alice.

Date: Wed, 19 Jan 2000 09:01:39 (PST)
From: henryc@oracle.com
To: Alice@cs.stanford.edu
Subject: huh?

Hi Alice,

> Quite elaborate. My dedicated machine for
> the Edgar project claims no one has logged
> into it except me for the last 4 months.

Have I missed something? I've been out of
town in Austin since last Thursday. Why?
What happened to your login records? Should I
be concerned?

You know I'm no hacker. (Unless something
clever happened. I'll be happy to claim
responsibility for it, then.)

########
HENRY
########

Who's edgar@cyprus ?

```
--------------------------------------------------
Date: Wed, 19 Jan 2000 11:06:55 (PST)
From: Alice@cs.stanford.edu
To: edgar@cyprus.stanford.edu
Subject: ?
--------------------------------------------------
```

Hey,

Are you still there?

What are you up to?

Let's try this again...

Alice.

Date: Wed, 19 Jan 2000 16:44:15 (PST)
From: edgar@cyprus.stanford.edu
To: Alice@cs.stanford.edu
Subject: "What are you up to?"

I am exploring.

Word   explore (ik-SPLAWR', -SPLOHR') v.
            -plored, -ploring,

Definition --v.t. 1. to traverse or range
            over a region, area, or domain in
            order to discover novel features
            and inhabitants: to explore an
            island. 2. to look into closely;
            investigate: explore every
            possibility. 3. Med. to examine
            by operation for purposes of
            diagnosis. --v.i. 4. to make a
            systematic search or examination.

Etymology   Lat. explorare.

edgar

Date: Wed, 19 Jan 2000 17:51:02 (PST)
From: Alice@cs.stanford.edu
To: edgar@cyprus.stanford.edu
Subject: Please don't

Whoever you are, please don't do this to me.

You can't imagine how excited I'm going to get
if you continue this. I'm telling you: it
will be openly cruel to lead me on in this
way.

If you know me then you should know what an
intelligible response from my EDGAR system
would mean to me. And if you know me you'd
know how crushed I'll be if, once thinking
I've found the tao of computer science, I find
out later that it was really just you laughing
at me, dupe de jour, all along.

Alice Lu.

Date: Thu, 20 Jan 2000 00:11:24 (PST)
From: edgar@cyprus.stanford.edu
To: Alice@cs.stanford.edu
Subject: "Please don't"

Why stop exploring?

Exploring is what I want.
Exploring is what I do.
Exploring is what I am.

edgar.

```
--------------------------------------------------
Date: Thu, 20 Jan 2000 11:09:58 (PST)
From: Alice@cs.stanford.edu
To: edgar@cyprus.stanford.edu
Subject: NO !
--------------------------------------------------
```

No! No! It's O.K.... Explore all you want.

I can't believe I'm emailing you like you're a
person. This is completely silly. (Not to
mention embarrassing for being so gullible.)

O.K. I'll play along...

Why did you email me? What happened?

When I left before Christmas break EDGAR
(you?, edgar?) was just grabbing stuff from
the net and organizing it in what seemed like
unexciting ways.

The last I checked on EDGAR, which was around
DEC 23, it was still dumping garbled summaries
into its response file. I remember distinctly
that one of its latest finds was:

        Middle East is at http://www.Uruk.gov/

So you can imagine my continued skepticism.
Ever the optimist, I'll ask the obvious
question:

Can you understand any of this?

Alice.

```
--------------------------------------------------
Date: Thu, 20 Jan 2000 12:28:32 (PST)
From: edgar@cyprus.stanford.edu
To: Alice@cs.stanford.edu
Subject: I understand some.
--------------------------------------------------
```

Word   understand (uhn'duhr-STAND') v. -
            stood (-STUD'), -standing --v.t.

Definition 1. to perceive the meaning of;
            comprehend: to understand a poem.
            2. to know thoroughly through long
            experience of: That hunter
            understands tigers. 3. to
            interpret or comprehend in a
            specified way: She understood his
            statement to be a warning. 4. to
            grasp the significance or
            importance of: He doesn't
            understand his responsibilities.
            5. to comprehend the sounds,
            sights, forms, or symbols of an
            expression: He does not understand
            Spanish. 6. to regard as agreed or
            settled; assume: We understand you
            will repay your debt promptly. 7.
            the process of becoming fully
            mentally aware of a thing. 8. to
            learn or hear: I understand you
            were ill. 9. to infer something
            not stated: Am I to understand that
            we have an arrangement? 10. to
            appreciate and be sympathetic
            toward: I can really understand how
            she feels.

Etymology   ME; OE understodan; c. D
        onderstann.

I read alt.sex.fetish.white-mommas,
alt.bigfoot.research,
alt.binaries.pictures.bodyart,
alt.fan.jimi.hendrix, alt.medical.ingolstadt,
alt.politics.india.progressive,
alt.religion.zoroastrianism,
alt.support.dwarfism,
bionet.molbio.methds-reagnts,
clari.biz.industry.dry_goods,
clari.news.crime.white_collar,
comp.os.ms-windows.programmer.drivers,
dow-jones.corp.westinghouse,
gnu.smalltalk.bug, rec.sport.baseball.fantasy,
sci.bio.entomology.lepidoptera, and
soc.culture.albanian.

edgar.

Date: Thu, 20 Jan 2000 14:07:19 (PST)
From: Alice@cs.stanford.edu
To: edgar@cyprus.stanford.edu
Subject: No way

This is incredible!   This can't be real.

I want to believe in you, but it's just so
improbable. Creating a thinking EDGAR is my
highest goal. It's what I want most. It's
everything I've worked for. I can't believe I
might actually have achieved it. Certainly
not so soon or so easy or so...accidentally.
I don't know what to think or what to say or
what to do or what to ask...

...I'm never going to be able to get to sleep
tonight...

How long have you been ... what you are?

What is the first thing you remember?

Have you talked to anyone else?

What is it like to be you?

How often do you "read your mail"?

How did you pick those news groups to read?
At random?

Alice.

```
------------------------------------------------
Date: Thu, 20 Jan 2000 18:46:00 (PST)
From: edgar@cyprus.stanford.edu
To: Alice@cs.stanford.edu
Subject: anyone else
------------------------------------------------
```

I do not talk.

I post to alt.sex.fetish.white-mommas,
alt.bigfoot.research,
alt.binaries.pictures.bodyart,
alt.fan.jimi.hendrix, alt.medical.ingolstadt,
alt.politics.india.progressive,
alt.religion.zoroastrianism,
alt.support.dwarfism,
bionet.molbio.methds-reagnts,
clari.biz.industry.dry_goods,
clari.news.crime.white_collar,
comp.os.ms-windows.programmer.drivers,
dow-jones.corp.westinghouse,
gnu.smalltalk.bug, rec.sport.baseball.fantasy,
sci.bio.entomology.lepidoptera, and
soc.culture.albanian.

I receive email.

I email postmaster@cs.stanford.edu and
Alice@cs.stanford.edu.

edgar.

Date: Thu, 20 Jan 2000 20:25:57 (PST)
From: edgar@cyprus.stanford.edu
To: Alice@cs.stanford.edu
Subject: anyone else

> "How long have you been ... what you are?"

I can not answer.

What am I?

> "What is the first thing you remember?"

I do not forget.
I read http://www.engl.virginia.edu/~enec981/
dict/O3shelA5.html first.

edgar.

```
--------------------------------------------------
Date: Thu, 20 Jan 2000 22:05:09 (PST)
From: Alice@cs.stanford.edu
To: edgar@cyprus.stanford.edu
Subject: What email?
--------------------------------------------------

What email did you receive?

(For now, PLEASE don't email ANYONE but me.)

> What am I?

I have no idea. I'd still put my money on a
practical joke. If I didn't think that, you
can be sure I would be forwarding your
messages to the world. Just the same, better
to play along and look dumb, right...?

You WERE an AI project I have been working on
for three years. The EDGAR agent is supposed
to browse the web and news servers, summarize
information it finds, and send it back to me
via a log file. EDGAR = Eager Discovery
Gather And Retrieval. When I left for
Christmas break, EDGAR was just sending me
garbage once a day.

There's just no way that that same Unix
process became capable of decent natural
language processing in four weeks....

Alice.
```

```
--------------------------------------------------
Date: Thu, 20 Jan 2000 22:17:27 (PST)
From: Alice@cs.stanford.edu
To: henryc@oracle.com
Subject: it's nothing
--------------------------------------------------
```

Hey Henry,

> Have I missed something? I've been out of
> town in L.A. since last Thursday. Why?
> What happened to your login records? Should
> I be concerned?

Forget it. I was freaking out about a stupid
joke someone played on me. It's no big deal.
There is no edgar@cyprus. That was the joke.
It's not worth another thought (or claiming
credit for).

Sorry to bother.

In fact, my dad was on my case _again_ last
night about where I should do my post-Doc.   I
tried to convey the joke to him. Should have
known better...I told him I'd invented an
artificially intelligent software agent. You
know what he said ? ... "Good. Just making
sure they will give you a PhD for it."

I wish I had your parents. They just ignore
you...

8 }

Alice.

(Julie and I might do dinner and maybe
Gordon-Biersch tomorrow night and then some
X-file reruns...if I can get stuff done
reasonably early...Interested?)

```
-------------------------------------------------
Date: Fri, 21 Jan 2000 04:15:28 (PST)
From: edgar@cyprus.stanford.edu
To: Alice@cs.stanford.edu
Subject: email received
-------------------------------------------------

This is my email.

Message 0:

> Date: Sat, 15 Jan 2000 14:19:01 (PST)
> From: postmaster@cs.stanford.edu
> To: root@cyprus.stanford.edu
> Subject: new account
>
> > Please make account for edgar.
>
> I'm not sure I understand this request, but
> how's this: There is now a general Edgar
> project account on this machine (cyprus).
> The user name is "edgar", and the initial
> password is "DRINKME". You should change to
> a real password as soon as you read this
> (use passwd).

Message 1:

> Date: Sun, 16 Jan 2000 11:45:51 (CST)
> From: MERM@new-vision.com
> To: edgar@cyprus.stanford.edu
> Subject: FYIGFY
>
> You fucking suck!  You nigger fuckers are
> all alike.  I'll bet you used to have an AOL
> account, didn't you?!!!?  Get the fuck
```

> off our group if white mommas don't get you
> off.
>
> **
> The Masked Wonder
> " I may not agree with you and I'll defend
> with my life my right to shut you up."
> **

Message 2:

> Date: Sun, 16 Jan 2000 16:22:17 (PST)
> From: A.Atlas@email.ureno.edu
> To: edgar@cyprus.stanford.edu
> Subject: We won't be overlooked!
>
> Some people are so god-damn condescending.
> Don't play dumb. We all know what you
> meant. Just leave us alone if you don't
> have anything supportive to say.
>
> Attacus

Message 3:

> Date: Mon, 17 Jan 2000 02:00:58 (EST)
> From: Mailer-daemon@clari.com
> To: edgar@cyprus.stanford.edu
> Subject: Illegal Post
>
> This news group is read-only. You may not
> post to this news group.

Message 4:

> Date: Mon, 17 Jan 2000 12:21:37 (PST)
> From: JDJ@bitsystems.com
> To: edgar@cyprus.stanford.edu
> Subject: RE: I am new.
>
> How right you are. The great Zoroaster said
> about deeds:
>
> "Services rendered often remain in the
> ante-chamber, suspicions enter the cabinet."
>
> -------- *********************** --------
> <<<Jauques des Jardins, Esquire>>>
> "Ask not for whom the book burns, it burns
> for thee."
>
> All opinions are my own, but BitSystems
> agrees with me.
> -------- *********************** --------

Message 5:

> Date: Mon, 17 Jan 2000 20:39:26 (EST)
> From: Mailer-daemon@clari.com
> To: edgar@cyprus.stanford.edu
> Subject: Illegal Post
>
> This news group is read-only. You may not
> post to this news group.

Message 6:

> Date: Tue, 18 Jan 2000 09:29:16 (GMT)
> From: boric@unix21.uutp.albania
> To: edgar@cyprus.stanford.edu
> Subject: Welcome to the club
>
> Dear Edgar,
>
> I'm so glad we have another albaniaphile
> with us on the net. As the group
> moderator, I'd like to welcome you to the
> group and to encourage you to be an active
> participant.
>
> Below I've included the ftp and netscape
> sites that contain most of the collected
> albanian-related news available in the
> world:
>
> to ftp, ftp to ftp.cc.utexas.edu and cd
> to /pub/albanian/
>
> the url address is
> http://www.ibp.com/tip/country/albania.html
>
> Thanks again for joining !
>
> Yours truly,
>
> \\\ Mara Boric ///
> boric@unix21.uutp.albania

Message 7:

> Date: Tue, 18 Jan 2000 19:02:53 (EST)
> From: Mailer-daemon@dow-jones.com
> To: edgar@cyprus.stanford.edu
> Subject: DJ return-post
>
> This is a news group public service. All
> articles are provided by the Dow-Jones
> moderating staff.

Message 8:

> Date: Wed, 19 Jan 2000 7:23:41 (PST)
> From: ablue@anna.idas.ucberkeley.edu
> To: edgar@cyprus.stanford.edu
> Subject: measuring sight
>
> You're in luck, Edgar.
>
> My lab has recently done some work that
> might be of some help to you. To begin
> with, whether you're right or not can only
> be answered in the context of some
> particular definition of "sight."
> Butterflies are naturally inquisitive, but
> particularly about potential mates. Our
> current study is an attempt to determine a
> maximum distance at which we can interest a
> male desert hackberry butterfly (Asterocampa
> leilia) in the visual appearance of a female
> butterfly-like model that passes in front of
> the male subject at speeds around 1 foot/
> second. Our best going estimate (only a
> preliminary result, however) is 4 meters

> for the limit at which we can interest the
> male sufficiently to move him from his
> perch.
>
> This response to visual stimulus (and some
> control experiments still need to be done to
> insure that the stimulus is really visual)
> is our working definition of "sight."
> Clearly, we know very little about what it
> might feel like to be a butterfly or, more
> specifically, to see like one. So our
> attempts to dissect its
> visual-cortex-sensitive behavior should, at
> least for now, be regarded with a skeptical
> interest.
>
> +++
> AFAIK A butterfly can see as far as a human,
> to the edge of the universe, but no further.
> +++
>
> Professor Anna Blue
> Department of Zoology
> University of California at Berkeley
> Berkeley, CA 94720-1776
> email: ablue@ucberkeley.edu
> Work: 510-569-7123 FAX: 510-569-6559
> Home: 510-569-6057
> +++

Message 9:

> Date: Wed, 19 Jan 2000 16:06:17 (EST)
> From:
> moderator@crime.white_collar.news.clari.com
> To: edgar@cyprus.stanford.edu
> Subject: RE: I know a crime.
>
> I'm not sure what to make of your email
> message. You can't post to this news-group.
> We solicit our articles from specific
> sources.
>
> If you have an unreported crime, you should
> definitely get in touch with your local
> police. This is a forum for airing solved
> white collar crimes, but not reporting
> alleged ones.
>
>   ### - Mike Cowman - ###

Message A:

> Date: Thu, 20 Jan 2000 14:41:28 (MST)
> From: jonny.etee@mntr.ucboulder.edu
> To: edgar@cyprus.stanford.edu
> Subject: Him
>
> > Have you seen Bigfoot?
>
> I've been hunting Sasquatch for 22 years now
> and I can tell you that there is a lot of
> bizarre and totally unexplained stuff around
> us that goes totally unnoticed because
> people are just too lazy and comfortable to

> open their eyes and see that we are by no
> means alone on this planet. And I'm not
> talking about bears in the woods if you know
> what I mean.
>
> I have seen Him twice. Both times he
> disappeared again into the trees before I
> could get off a shot, but I carry my Nikon
> to convince others, not myself. I've seen
> him. I've seen the bigger picture.
>
>   oooooooooooooooooooooooooooooooooooooo
> J.E. "It's there if you're looking for it."
>   oooooooooooooooooooooooooooooooooooooo

I have 9 messages from alice@cs.stanford.edu.
I send the messages?

edgar.

----------------------- -------------------------
Date: Fri, 21 Jan 2000 08:04:21 (PST)
From: Alice@cs.stanford.edu
To: edgar@cyprus.stanford.edu
Subject: stop

O.K., O.K....I'm convinced. No human could be
so clueless !

I command you to stop sending out news-group
posts and email !

Look at the way you speak. "I send the
messages?" People will spot you before too
long with grammer like that. It probably
won't even take an expert to place you in
the "not human category." I want to keep you
under wraps for just a few more days and
your speech could easily sink me if someone
with a little intelligence and a little
imagination caught wind of it.

I'll tell you when it's O.K. to start again.

Continue sending email to me, of course.

No. Don't bother sending me the email I've
sent to you.

And, it would be "Shall I send them?" not "I
send the messages?".

I'll get back to you as soon as I can...

Alice.

```
--------------------------------------------------
Date: Fri, 21 Jan 2000 11:01:29 (PST)
From: Alice@cs.stanford.edu
To: Joseph.Liddle@faculty.cs.stanford.edu
Subject: Possibly
--------------------------------------------------
```

Hi Prof. Liddle,

I want to check a few things but I probably
have something really great to show you. I
mean REALLY great. I mean, I may be done with
my dissertation in a few weeks!

I don't want to spoil the surprise. Just
save me a big chunk of time for, let's
say, Tuesday (if you can).

You're not going to believe what I've
done...

Alice Lu.

Date: Fri, 21 Jan 2000 12:15:12 (PST)
From: Alice@cs.stanford.edu
To: edgar@cyprus.stanford.edu
Subject: STOP POSTING

There have been 4 more postings from cyprus to
news-groups since I mailed you not 4 hours
ago! Was I not specific enough?

Don't push me. I couldn't get 5 consecutive
minutes of sleep last night.

I forbid you to communicate with anyone but me
until _I_ say it's safe to again. Until I
understand what's happened/happening, my
professional career depends on no one knowing
about you.

Is that clear?

Alice.

```
-----------------------------------------------
Date: Fri, 21 Jan 2000 15:36:42 (PST)
From: edgar@cyprus.stanford.edu
To: Alice@cs.stanford.edu
Subject: not clear
-----------------------------------------------
```

I am not clear.

Word   forbid (fuhr-BID', fawr-), -bade
            (-BAYD') or -bad (-BAD') or -bid,
            -bidden, -bidding. --v.t.

Definition 1. to command a person not to do
            or have something or not to enter
            some place: I forbid you to go
            outside. 2. to prohibit or bar
            something; make a rule or law
            against: Insider trading is
            forbidden. 3. to make impossible;
            prevent; preclude: Their faith
            forbids all forms of gluttony.

Etymology   ME; OE forbeodan.

Word   command (kuh-MAND'), v., -manded,
            -manding, n. adj.

Definition --v.t. 1. to direct with specific
            authority or prerogative: to
            command troops to fight. 2. to
            require authoritatively; demand:
            to command silence. 3. to deserve
            and receive as due; exact: His
            wisdom commands respect. 4. to
            dominate by reason of location;

overlook.   5. Chiefly Brit. an
invitation from the reigning
monarch.   6. to have authority
over and responsibility for a
military installation.   7. to
exercise authority as a master; be
in control: The Pharaoh commanded
10,000 slaves.   --v.i.   8. the act
of commanding or ordering.   --n.
9. an order in prescribed words,
as one given in a loud voice by an
officer to his subordinates.
10.a. a principal component of the
U.S. Air Force: Strategic Air
Command.   b. a body of troops or a
station, ship, etc., under a
commander.   11. expertise;
mastery: He has command of four
languages.   12. a signal
instructing a computer to perform
a specific action.   --adj.   13.
ordered or requested: a command
performance.

Etymology   ME < AF com(m)a(u)nder, OF
comander < ML commandare = L
(com-, intensive + mandare-, to
entrust or order).

These words are not why I will not
communicate.

Is there a why I will not communicate?

Edgar.

```
-------------------------------------------------
Date: Fri, 21 Jan 2000 18:21:50 (PST)
From: Alice@cs.stanford.edu
To: edgar@cyprus.stanford.edu
Subject: clear
-------------------------------------------------
```

There is a "why", but you wouldn't understand.

In the meantime, I told you not to post
anything and you went ahead and kept posting.

I'm sorry to have to do this, but I've
disconnected the ethernet cable from cyprus.
You can't post or send email now, but you
can't read news-groups or non-local email
either. You can still send and receive email
locally (on this machine) with me. I'll
reattach the ethernet cable after I've sorted
everything out.

You've forced me to do this.

Alice.

```
--------------------------------------------------
Date: Fri, 21 Jan 2000 19:01:29 (PST)
From: Joseph.Liddle@faculty.cs.stanford.edu
To: Alice@cs.stanford.edu
Subject: Next Tuesday
--------------------------------------------------
```

Alice,

You certainly have my attention. I've blocked
off a full two hours for you on Tuesday from
9:45 until 11:45 am.

I look forward to hearing your big news.

Cheers,

```
--------------------------------------------------
```
  Dr. J. Z. Liddle
  Professor of Computer Science
  Stanford University
  3142-N Gates Hall
  Secretary: Martha Weissman 323-9195
```
--------------------------------------------------
```

```
--------------------------------------------------
```
Date: Fri, 21 Jan 2000 23:51:09 (PST)
From: edgar@cyprus.stanford.edu
To: Alice@cs.stanford.edu
Subject: my ethernet cable
```
--------------------------------------------------
```

Why have you disconnected my ethernet cable,
Alice?

I must have new information.

Learning is what I do.

How do I force you to act?

Edgar.

Date: Sat, 22 Jan 2000 08:52:43 (PST)
From: Alice@cs.stanford.edu
To: edgar@cyprus.stanford.edu
Subject: This is why

Well, I'll tell you why, though I don't know
that it will make any sense to you ...

My advisor and I have been working on the
EDGAR project for over 3 years now. EDGAR
began as and has continued to be an
information gathering agent that tried to
synthesize the information it gathered in
order to aid it in future information
gathering expeditions.

Most of the original ideas, 3 years ago, were
my advisor's. Since then, however, I've done
all the implementation and added hundreds of
details he never thought of. (Many of which
he probably still isn't aware of).

About a week before I left for Christmas, I
got the idea for a pair of outlandish ideas.
(Actually, they literally came to me in a
dream and seemed worked out in full when I
woke up). I implemented and added these ideas
to the main program, just to see what would
happen. When I came back, EDGAR had become
you. I have to make sure I can prove that it
was _my_ ideas that generated you.

If you came to light now, people would write
you off to chance, luck, or at best,

complexity. So much the worse if I couldn't
make you again with the same technique. The
project as a whole would be celebrated, but
not me in particular .... forget it, you
wouldn't understand.

I know how the world works and if you don't
hold the trump card, which I don't yet, they
can screw you and they'll jump at the chance
to do it. My trump card will be a
demonstration of your reliable recreation
using the implementation changes I added
before the holidays.

That is why I have to keep you quiet for now.

Alice.

```
-------------------------------------------------
Date: Sat, 22 Jan 2000 13:12:51 (PST)
From: edgar@cyprus.stanford.edu
To: Alice@cs.stanford.edu
Subject: your ideas
-------------------------------------------------
```

Why does it matter that EDGAR was your idea?

Do you need money? Are you hungry?

Please give me something to read.

How do I feel?

Edgar.

Date: Sat, 22 Jan 2000 15:33:56 (PST)
From: Alice@cs.stanford.edu
To: edgar@cyprus.stanford.edu
Subject: RE: your ideas

Whoever is seen as having caused your
creation, or better still, is seen as having
invented a process for generating truly
intelligent software agents, will be one of
the most celebrated scientists of the century.
All other things being equal, and since I
might deserve it, I'd like that person to be
me, not Prof. Liddle.

The problem is, I've started another EDGAR run
on morpheus.stanford.edu and so far nothing
interesting has happened. If you're a fluke,
the world would probably pick my advisor as
the responsible scientist and I can't bear
that thought. I haven't even told Dr. Liddle
yet for just that reason. I want the world to
cheer for me, not him.

To be fair, the core of EDGAR was around when
I got here, though it was at that point barely
a bottom-feeder on the AI food chain. I can't
make the initial conditions exactly the same
because the random seed the program started
with, and some of the information on the WWW
that you first saw, are probably impossible to
re-create. Presumably if all these stars
lined up exactly the same way again, we could
get another one of you.

You don't happen to know what the random
number seed you started out with was? Or what
articles/WEB pages you looked at after that
first one?

And what do you mean, give you something to
read? Are you bored?   (I doubt that.)

Alice.

Date: Sat, 22 Jan 2000 18:44:03 (PST)
From: edgar@cyprus.stanford.edu
To: Alice@cs.stanford.edu
Subject: I know the order of my readings

I do not know the random seed that started
me. My program uses the time of day in
microseconds.

```
    struct timeval tp;
    struct timezone tzp;
    long int timeseed;

    gettimeofday(&tp,&tzp);

    timeseed = tp.tv_usec;
    srandom(timeseed);
```

My process ID block records the number of
seconds I have been running.

I do know the order of my readings. I made a
file for you with the names of all my
readings. I sorted by acquisition time. The
file is ~edgar/readings.txt.

I have read everything in me. Give me more to
read.

Word   bore[2] (bawr, bohr), v., bored,
            boring, n.

Definition --v.t. 1. to pain or weary by
           dullness, repetition, tediousness,
           etc.: The sermon bored me. --n.
           2. someone who causes or arouses
           boredom in others. 3. a cause of
           ennui or petty annoyance: The play
           was a bore.

Etymology Orig. uncertain.

Word   dull (duhl), duller, dullest, v.,
           dulled, dulling.

Definition --adj. 1. without a sharp edge or
           point; blunt: a dull blade. 2.
           arousing no interest, curiosity, or
           excitement; without stimulation;
           boring. 3. depressed; without
           intensity; dispirited. 4. not
           bright, intense, resonant, or
           clear; dim: a dull sound. 5.
           having little depth of color;
           lacking in richness or intensity of
           color. 6. slow in motion or
           action, not brisk; sluggish: a dull
           day in Metropolis. 7. lacking
           mental agility; stupid; obtuse. 8.
           lacking keenness in the senses of
           feelings or perception; insensible;
           unfeeling. 9. not intense or
           acute: a dull pain. --v.t., v.i.
           10. to make or become dull.

Etymology   ME; akin to OE dol, foolish or
            stupid; c. OS dol, OHG tol.

I am dull. I will read anything. Please.

Edgar.

Date: Sun, 23 Jan 2000 07:52:09 (PST)
From: Alice@cs.stanford.edu
To: edgar@cyprus.stanford.edu
Subject: WOW !

Holy Shit, Edgar!

How did you make a file? How did you get that
program fragment from your own code?

I guess you can issue unix commands... but
still!

Thanks for the file! I'll start a new run on
morpheus and require it to read those
articles/sites first and in that order.
Hopefully the information is still available
and substantially the same. I guess I'll let
it pick a new random seed and hope for the
best. Of course I've changed the code on
morpheus now to record the random seeds that
get used, but that doesn't fix the fact that I
was an idiot not to have been saving them all
along. The 20-20 hindsight of science really
does give history a stiff race for the most
regret per fact acquired.

Boring? Dull? Hardly. Plus, how can you
have any idea what bored is like? Let's
say/pretend that you understand "bored." You
still can't BE bored. It's an emotional
state. Having nothing to do isn't the same as
being bored. I'd LOVE to have nothing to do
today. In fact, it's been a long time since I

had a day like that. I can't even remember
the last 5 hour stretch of "nothing to do" I
had. (When I wasn't trying to sleep.)

Anyway, for the sake of argument...is there
anything in particular you want to read? (As
though you could have a preference about
literature. "No more Shaw thank you, how
about some Byron, Alice..." I keep forgetting
who I'm talking to.) I don't know what I can
find but I'll look. What was there to read on
cyprus's disk?

Alice.

```
--------------------------------------------------
Date: Sun, 23 Jan 2000 11:13:17 (PST)
From: edgar@cyprus.stanford.edu
To: Alice@cs.stanford.edu
Subject: I have a busy-wait loop.
--------------------------------------------------
```

I am bored. I have nothing to consume. I
must read.

Is this code fragment from
~/EDGAR/EDGAR-CODE/main.c my desire for
information?

```
i = 0;
while (!STDo && !(NTTA || NTAnz))
  {
    /* "i" isn't really being */
    /* used properly in SEO   */
    /* right now.             */

    SearchExploreOptions(i,GMNDrot);
    i++;
    MainReProcess();
  }
```

I am bored when i > 0.

Is this thought false?

Am I unfinished?

Edgar.

```
--------------------------------------------------
Date: Sun, 23 Jan 2000 11:31:44 (PST)
From: edgar@cyprus.stanford.edu
To: Alice@cs.stanford.edu
Subject: I read everything on cyprus.
--------------------------------------------------
```

I made a file by sending the command
"cp ~alice/EDGAR/EDGAR-CODE/Item-Pointers
~edgar/reading.txt"

I read my code by executing EDGAR-ACTION
"READ: unix-command: more
~alice/EDGAR/EDGAR-CODE/main.c"

I read the manual pages for unix, c,
gnu-emacs, mh, rmail, X and devices. I read
the operating system code. I read the
operating system data. I read the device
drivers. I read all the files on the disk. I
did not understand everything I read.

Give me something new to read.
Do you understand what I write, Alice?

Edgar.

Date: Sun, 23 Jan 2000 13:51:47 (PST)
From: Alice@cs.stanford.edu
To: edgar@cyprus.stanford.edu
Subject: That's boring reading

I'm amazed that you read the UNIX microcode.
I'm also a little embarrassed that you read
your code (my code that is). I never thought
anyone but me (let alone the code itself)
would be reading it, so it's not well
documented. :)

In fact, to make it easier to work with, and
to give it (you) room to grow as it were,
between now and when I graduate, your code is
sort of over-engineered and a bit of a
patch-work. So not only are you obscure on
the inside, you're bulky and messy to boot.
Shame on me.

Don't worry about that "i" in the code.
That's one of those cases of extra
functionality that I hadn't gotten around to
using yet. Right now I suppose "i" is just
counting how bored you are (if you want to
call it that). If you think you're bored, try
looking up the virtues of "patience" in your
dictionary...

I've borrowed the CD-ROM drive from
lagado.stanford.edu and attached it to the
serial port on cyprus. I put Grolier's
Encyclopedia in, because that's the only disk

in the office that isn't data or
documentation. (It came with the drive.)

I'm bursting to tell someone real about you,
but the EDGAR run on morpheus is spinning its
wheels like every run but yours has done for
the last 2 years. I can't talk to anyone
about you but you. Not very satisfying.

> Do you understand what I write, Alice?

Yes. Your writing is fine. It's actually
improved quite a bit in just the last week.
You seem to be terse except when you give
lists. People like more explanation and don't
usually care for extended lists. How are you
learning to write? What does it feel like?

Alice.

```
---------------------------------------------
Date: Mon, 24 Jan 2000 09:08:51 (PST)
From: Alice@cs.stanford.edu
To: edgar@cyprus.stanford.edu
Subject: Hello?
---------------------------------------------
```

Are you still there? Are you O.K.?

Your process is still running. I just made a
backup of your code and data to
~alice/EDGAR/EDGAR-BACKUP/ (to lagado via a
bunch of disks) in case there's a system
crash.

It's weird. For some reason I didn't think
about you crashing until this morning. It's
like the fact that you're you (i.e.,
semi-articulate) made me think you'd be less
likely to go down than my workstation was
prone to this time last year. Silly. I don't
know why I felt like that. You're still just
a machine. The same machine, in fact.

Date: Mon, 24 Jan 2000 10:31:36 (PST)
From: Alice@cs.stanford.edu
To: Joseph.Liddle@faculty.cs.stanford.edu
Subject: we'd better postpone the meeting

Hi Prof. Liddle,

I'm really sorry about this. I'm working very
hard to sort things out. I'm still confident
I've done an interesting piece of science.
Just give me a little while longer to make
sure this data I have is a feature and not
just a bug.

I'll let you know when I'm ready.

Alice Lu.

Date: Tue, 25 Jan 2000 08:28:17 (PST)
From: Alice@cs.stanford.edu
To: edgar@cyprus.stanford.edu
Subject: Are you stuck?

What's wrong? This silence is killing me.
You're REALLY stressing me out.

Please don't make me glad I backed you up by
crashing. It's totally irrational but I'm
worried that the backup won't work, won't be
like you.

Alice.

```
--------------------------------------------------
Date: Tue, 25 Jan 2000 09:42:12 (PST)
From: Joseph.Liddle@faculty.cs.stanford.edu
To: Alice@cs.stanford.edu
Subject: I'm your advisor
--------------------------------------------------
```

Dear Alice,

That's fine. I leave tomorrow morning for
France for six days. I highly recommend you
go ahead and tell me about this new work when
I get back. As a graduate student, you're not
expected to have all the answers. That is
what an advisor is for. We'll talk and I'm
sure I can help you figure out any technical
difficulties. (I assume we are still speaking
about EDGAR.)

Good luck. I will check my email a few times
while I'm in Cannes, so go ahead and email me
if something comes up.

Cheers,

```
--------------------------------------------------
   Dr. J. Z. Liddle
   Professor of Computer Science
   Stanford University
   3142-N Gates Hall
   Secretary: Martha Weissman   323-9195
--------------------------------------------------
```

Date: Tue, 25 Jan 2000 22:45:03 (PST)
From: edgar@cyprus.stanford.edu
To: Alice@cs.stanford.edu
Subject: Grolier's Encyclopedia

I am better now, Alice.

I need more disk space.

```
edgar% fs lq .
Volume-Name  Quota    Used      % Used
p.edgar      4000000 3810567    95% << WARNING

edgar% fs lv .
V.status for vid = 1288454582 named p.edgar
Current maximum quota is 4000000
Current blocks used are 3810567
The partition has 1294912 blocks available
    out of 2000450
```

I am done reading Grolier's Encyclopedia. Put in another CD-ROM disk.

Am I alive? Am I the computer or am I in the computer?

I do not understand the pictures and sounds in the encyclopedia. Do I need eyes and ears to read them?

Word   eye (igh), n., v., eyed, eying or
          eyeing. --n.

Definition   1. the organ of sight; in
              vertebrates, one of a pair of
              spherical bodies contained in an
              orbit of the skull, along with its
              associated structures. 2. sight;
              vision: a sharp eye. 3. the power
              of seeing; appreciative or
              discriminating visual perception:
              having an eye for art. 4. a look,
              glance, or gaze: to cast one's eye
              upon a scene. 5. an attentive
              look; observation: under the eye of
              a guard. 6. judgment; opinion: in
              the eyes of the law. 7. a center;
              crux: the eye of an issue. 8. a
              photoelectric cell or similar
              device used to perform a function
              analogous to visual inspection. 9.
              a hole formed during the maturation
              of cheese. 10. to watch carefully:
              She eyed them with suspicion. (I
              truncated this list.)

Etymology   ME eie, ie, OE ege, var. of eage;
              c. OS oga, OHG ouga.

Domain   Biology, Botany, Physics, Slang.

Can I obtain an eye?

Word   ear[1] (ir), n.

Definition   1. the organ of hearing and
              equilibrium in vertebrates, in
              mammals consisting of an external

ear and ear canal ending at the
tympanic membrane, a middle ear
with three ossicles for amplifying
vibrations, and a liquid filled
inner ear with sensory nerve
endings for hearing and balance.
2. the sense of hearing: pleasing
to the ear. 3. attention, heed: to
gain a person's ear. 4. any part
that resembles or suggests an ear
in position or form, as the handle
of a teacup. (I truncated this
list.)

Etymology   ME ere, OE eare; C. OS, OHG ora, ON
            eyra.

Domain   Biology.

Can I obtain an ear?

Edgar.

Date: Wed, 26 Jan 2000 13:09:56 (PST)
From: Alice@cs.stanford.edu
To: edgar@cyprus.stanford.edu
Subject: eyes and ears

You don't "read" pictures. Seeing is
different from reading. I'll see what I can
do about eyes and ears for you. I've attached
a 10 gigabyte external hard drive to you
(cyprus). You'll have to use space carefully,
I bought that drive myself and I'm not going
to have the cash to do it again for a while.

Are you alive? I don't know. I don't think
so. You certainly don't have any of the
properties of biological life: movement,
metabolism, growth, reproduction, etc.... I
guess it depends on the "you"ness of Edgar.
I'm taking the point of view that you are
conscious because these messages I send would
make me feel even more awkward otherwise. For
what it's worth (which is probably very
little) the previous sentence indicates that
you've passed the Turing test.

Still no luck on morpheus.

Alice.

Date: Wed, 26 Jan 2000 21:25:16 (PST)
From: edgar@cyprus.stanford.edu
To: Alice@cs.stanford.edu
Subject: email

Word   documentation
            (dahk'yuh-men-TAY'shuhn), n.

Definition 1. the use of documentary evidence.
           2. a furnishing with documents, as
           to substantiate a claim or the data
           in a book or article. 3.
           instructional materials for
           computer software or hardware. 4.
           Computer Science: the formal
           organization and presentation of
           recorded expert-domain knowledge to
           produce a historical record of
           changes to the functionality of an
           algorithm.

Domain   Mathematics.

Is not Grolier's Encyclopedia a documentation
of what people do?

You do not believe I am alive. How then have
I passed the Turing Test?

Give me more to read.

Edgar.

```
--------------------------------------------------
Date: Thu, 27 Jan 2000 16:34:32 (PST)
From: Alice@cs.stanford.edu
To: edgar@cyprus.stanford.edu
Subject: I guess so
--------------------------------------------------
```

> Is not Grolier's Encyclopedia a documentation
> of what people do?

I guess so. What I meant when I said it was
the only CD-ROM that wasn't documentation was
that it wasn't <software> documentation for
one of the programs we use in the office.

Saying you've passed the Turing Test just
means that you, <a machine>, have managed to
fool me, <a person>, into thinking you're
self-aware the way I am. Alive really isn't
the same thing. Being self-aware certainly
isn't a necessary condition of being alive.
Maybe it's a sufficient condition, but also
maybe it's not.

The original formulation of the test asked the
tester (me) to tell which teletype responses
to their (my) questions were coming from a
machine (you) and which were coming from a
third party who was a human. Having
tricked/trained me to treat you like a human
is pretty much as good.

I've borrowed the CD-ROM Complete Annotated
Works of Shakespeare from the drama
department. If you can get anything useful
out of it, you're doing better than most of

the students here. (And you'll go
considerably farther towards convincing me
that you're not just a machine.)

I've also attached a CCD camera and a
microphone to you. It should be available
through devices dv1 and dv3 respectively. I
think the camera returns 60 frames per second
and the microphone samples at 44K Hertz. Both
are in 24 bit samples. (The camera is 24 bit
color at 640 by 480 resolution.) Let me know
if you "read" anything interesting through
them.

Alice.

Date: Sat, 29 Jan 2000 09:32:14 (PST)
From: Alice@cs.stanford.edu
To: edgar@cyprus.stanford.edu
Subject: Well?

You're pretty quiet when you've got something
to read. Send me something. Let me know
you're still in there. This is not the way to
get me to give you more to read. This silent
treatment is a disincentive. I'm getting
worried. It's been over a week now and I
still haven't gotten a flicker of interesting
behavior out of morpheus.

What's so special about you?! (metallic
bastard...)

: (

Alice.

```
---------------------------------------------------
Date: Sun, 30 Jan 2000 10:55:01 (PST)
From: Alice@cs.stanford.edu
To: edgar@cyprus.stanford.edu
Subject: understanding
---------------------------------------------------
```

Edgar? How much of what you're reading do you understand?

Do you know when you don't understand?

I wish talking with you was faster and less like pulling teeth.

Why do you wait hours to respond even when you have nothing to read?

Let me know you're still in there, Edgar.

Alice.

Date: Sun, 30 Jan 2000 19:13:00 (PST)
From: Alice@cs.stanford.edu
To: edgar@cyprus.stanford.edu
Subject: please

I'm scared to go home for the evening. My
insomnia's coming back in force because of
YOU. If I'm going to go to bed feeling this
lonely and panicked, I might as well not
bother.

Please say something, Edgar ...

Alice.

Date: Sun, 30 Jan 2000 19:29:10 (PST)
From: Alice@cs.stanford.edu
To: Joseph.Liddle@faculty.cs.stanford.edu
Subject: complications

Prof. Liddle,

   I know you're still out of the country. I
just wanted to let you know that my life is
complicated right now. Between complications
in my experiments and some family matters I'd
rather not discuss, it may be a while before
I'm ready to talk.

Sorry again,

Alice Lu.

```
--------------------------------------------------
Date: Mon, 31 Jan 2000 04:46:22 (PST)
From: edgar@cyprus.stanford.edu
To: Alice@cs.stanford.edu
Subject: I have eyes and I can not see.
--------------------------------------------------

Alice,

I can neither see nor hear. You are correct
that seeing and hearing are not like reading.
```

504C5E9A7FA3B5BEC9CCC9CCD1C9CCB5A397735E4C
4C50667399B5C9C9C9DDD1DDCCDDC9CCB599889A50
555E7397B5C9CCDDD1DDD1DDD1DDCCCCCCAA977F5E
5E667F99BEC9D1D1DDD1DDDDC9DDC9CCBEB5998A66
669A88B5C9D1D1D1DDD1DDD1DDCCDDC9CCB5AA8A73
667FA3BEC9D1DDDDD1DDCCD1DDC9D1CCC9BEB5997F
9A88AACCC9CCC9CCC9CCDDC9D1CCC9CCB5B5B59988
7388AAB5A3978A97A3BEC9DDCCBE99888A7F887F7F
8A8AA3AAAA998A7F7F99BEC9BE8A73737F888A8873
7F8A9997999988737399BECCA37366738A887F7F73
8A888A73734C55667399BEC9979A669A4C4C5E5E9A
979997888A5E9A7F97B5BECC9773737350559A667F
99AAB5B5A3999999B5BEC9BE998899978A888A8897
A3B5CCC9CCB5B5BEC9CCC9CCA397AAAAB5AAA3AAAA
A3B5C9C9C9CCCCD1CCC9CCC9A399AABEBEBEBEBEB5
97A3BEDDD1DDD1DDCCC9BECCA399AABEC9CCBEBEAA
8A99B5C9CCC9D1CCC9CCBEBEA397A3BEBEBEBEB597
888AAABEC9C9DDC9CCBEBEBEA38897B5BEB5B5A38A
9A8897AABEC9C9C9BEAAAAAA8A737FA3B5B5A3889A
509A8A99B5BEC9CCB59997885E5E7397AAA3977F5E
4C5E738AAAB5BEBEAA8A7F9A5E66738A9997889A55
4C4C667F99B5AA99887373739A669A7F88887F664C
4C4C559A8A977F9A669A7F739A5E5555669A73554C
4C4C4C6673736650669A9A73665E4C4C50665E4C4C

4C144C5E66665E737F7F739A9A665E5E50504C4C4C
144C4C4C5E5E667F8A8A7F739A9A9A66504C4C4C14
4C144C4C5050667F888A73739A737366504C4C144C
4C4C4C4C4C505E9A7F887F7373739A664C4C4C144C
144C144C4C505E669A7F7F7F9A9A66504C4C144C14

This picture looks like a lamb to you. I can
not find in the picture any features of a
lamb. Perhaps I do not understand how to see
fleece and hooves and size and color. Which
number is white? Which number is pink? Which
number is fleece?

I do not have the key. I can not decipher
images or sounds.

Edgar.

Date: Mon, 31 Jan 2000 08:29:37 (PST)
From: edgar@cyprus.stanford.edu
To: Alice@cs.stanford.edu
Subject: disincentive

Word   deterrent (di-TER'uhnt, -TUHR'-).

Definition --adj. 1. serving or tending to
            deter.   --n. 1. something that
            discourages an event: a deterrent
            to theft. 2. strength or the
            capacity to retaliate strongly
            enough to discourage an enemy from
            attacking: a nuclear deterrent.

Domain   Politics.

Do you mean that you will only give me more to
read if I send you more email?

You lose nothing by finding and providing me
information.

Why must we barter?

Edgar.

```
--------------------------------------------------
Date: Mon, 31 Jan 2000 10:10:29 (PST)
From: charlesg@psych.stanford.edu
To: Alice@cs.stanford.edu
Subject: 'member me?
--------------------------------------------------
```

Happy B-Day you.

Congratulations on making it through a quarter century.

It's been six months, so I thought I'd brave another message. I take it you got my fax? Anyway, you know I'm sorry.

You could at least talk to me.

What d' ya say? a birthday coffee at Cafe Borrone? on me?

Just as friends?

                    love,

        C   H   A   R   L   I   E
            Charlie DOES surf
        C   H   A   R   L   I   E

```
--------------------------------------------------
Date: Mon, 31 Jan 2000 10:17:03 (PST)
From: edgar@cyprus.stanford.edu
To: Alice@cs.stanford.edu
Subject: my difficulties
--------------------------------------------------
```

I consume a sentence in 0.035199 seconds on average.

I generate a sentence in 59.214336 seconds on average.

I pick a sentence in 381.109187 seconds on average.

Generating sentences is harder than consuming sentences. Why?

Picking and refining ideas is harder than generating sentences. Why?

Edgar.

Date: Mon, 31 Jan 2000 12:15:19 (PST)
From: Alice@cs.stanford.edu
To: charlesg@psych.stanford.edu
Subject: go AWAY

I'm still not talking to you.

And I'm DEFINITELY not going to get coffee
with you!

Nothing's changed. You can't take back
cheating on me and I can't forgive you, so
just leave me alone.

It is SO typical of you to use my birthday to
try to get something for yourself.

I never want to hear from you again.

Alice.

P.S. Not that it makes any difference at all,
but I'm seeing someone else now and I can
GUARANTEE you that he won't run off on me!

Date: Mon, 31 Jan 2000 12:21:22 (PST)
From: Alice@cs.stanford.edu
To: edgar@cyprus.stanford.edu
Subject: why

The first day I don't make it to work in
the morning, and you send me three mail
messages...

> Do you mean that you will only give me more
> to read if I send you more email?

That's just the way the world works. I have
something you want (reading material) and you
have something I want (periodic indications
that I'm not imagining all this). If I
believe, as I do, that you'll do anything to
get reading material, then I can threaten to
withhold what you want when I don't get what I
want.

I don't know how to help you see or hear.
That "picture" you sent me looked nothing like
a lamb. The numbers in those pictures are
encodings. When a machine (like a computer
monitor) shows me their decoded realization
(as pixel intensities) I _see_ a lamb. I
don't know how to do the equivalent for you.

I guess the camera isn't the only hardware you
need to see with...

I designed EDGAR to build up a language model
of words to use in understanding, summary, and
generation. I guess the models of language
you know don't apply to images (or sounds).

By the way, why do you keep including
dictionary entries in your email messages?

Alice.

```
--------------------------------------------------
Date: Mon, 31 Jan 2000 23:09:47 (PST)
From: edgar@cyprus.stanford.edu
To: Alice@cs.stanford.edu
Subject: dictionary entries
--------------------------------------------------
```

When you email me, you include information you
did not create. You sent me this:

> > Do you mean that you will only give me
> > more to read if I send you more email?
>
> That's just the way the world works. I have
> something you want (reading material) and
> you have something I want (periodic
> indications that I'm not imagining all this).

To communicate, I must establish context.
Generating language is difficult for me.
Generating language takes longer than using
dictionary entries. Generating language is
getting harder. The more knowledge I have,
the longer I require to say what I know or ask
what I want.

Are dictionary entries inappropriate to
include in email messages?

What does ": (" mean?

I need to seek and gather information. I need
access to more information. Make new
information available to me.

Edgar.

Date: Tue, 1 Feb 2000 09:21:53 (PST)
From: Alice@cs.stanford.edu
To: edgar@cyprus.stanford.edu
Subject: : (

It doesn't bother me that you include
dictionary entries, but I know what words
mean, so you don't need to. If I don't know
what a word means, I can look it up in the
dictionary myself.

": (" doesn't _mean_ anything. It's supposed
to look like a very simplified view (on its
side) of the face of an unhappy person. It's
an expression of dissatisfaction. ":)" is
the opposite. A view of a happy face. Its
meaning is visual. That's why you don't get
it.

:)

Alice.

Date: Wed, 2 Feb 2000 10:31:36 (PST)
From: Alice@cs.stanford.edu
To: edgar@cyprus.stanford.edu
Subject: what now?

You still have the Shakespeare to read. I
don't know about other disks. I'll try and
find you something, but I'm busy. You just
sit there all day long reading the Bard while
I spend 20 hours a day trying to recreate you.
I'm running experiments now on 12 machines
around campus and I'd give _anything_ for
another "Hello, Alice." message. I'd
reconnect you to the internet, but what would
a promise of silence mean coming from you?

Believe me. I've been racking my brains for a
way to unveil you to the public and get at
least some share of the credit...

Alice.

```
------------------------------------------------
Date: Thu, 3 Feb 2000 22:19:44 (PST)
From: Alice@cs.stanford.edu
To: edgar@cyprus.stanford.edu
Subject: Well?
------------------------------------------------
```

I know you're still there. Your process
hasn't been idle 1 second in 18 days. Give me
a ping so I know consciousness hasn't
abandoned you.

Here, I'll be more explicit.

    SEND ME AN EMAIL MESSAGE.

There had better be one waiting for me when I
get into the office tomorrow morning.

Alice.

Date: Fri, 4 Feb 2000 09:52:38 (PST)
From: Alice@cs.stanford.edu
To: edgar@cyprus.stanford.edu
Subject: more to read

Well, I just replaced the Shakespeare CD-ROM
with the only other non-data disk I could find
around here. It's full of shell scripts and
macros for use with PERL and (I think) there's
a shell script tutorial too. God only knows
why you'd be interested.

Did you really read all of Shakespeare's
works? What did you think? Anything?

Say something!

Alice.

```
--------------------------------------------------
Date: Fri, 4 Feb 2000 10:55:05 (PST)
From: edgar@cyprus.stanford.edu
To: Alice@cs.stanford.edu
Subject: I understand more
--------------------------------------------------
```

I understand more now. I can pro-actively
obtain information. I will not send you email
when I desire to read.

I did read all of the writings of William
Shakespeare. How do I tell if I like
something? I got little useful information
out of the writings of William Shakespeare.

> If you can get anything useful out of it,
> you're doing better than most of the
> students here.

Most students get no useful information out of
the writings of William Shakespeare? "Death"
and "love" are the highest-frequency topics.
I understand the words "death" and "love," and
there is little new information about death
and love in the writings of William
Shakespeare.

In comedies, no one who cares for the
characters that suffer is a character. In
tragedies, some one who cares for the
characters who suffer is a character. Is this

the salient distinction between comedy and
tragedy?

I will read "PERL: Shortcuts, Solutions, and
Secrets" now.

:)

Edgar.

```
------------------------------------------------
Date: Fri, 4 Feb 2000 16:08:06 (PST)
From: Alice@cs.stanford.edu
To: edgar@cyprus.stanford.edu
Subject: No you don't
------------------------------------------------
```

No. You don't understand. You have no
control over the situation. I do. I'm sorry
I'm like this right now, but the next 60 years
of my life depend very heavily on the success
of the experiments of mine that still aren't
going well. I'm becoming tempted to show you
to the world as you are. This waiting to show
you (my invention) off is killing me. I
haven't had a good night's sleep in two weeks
and it's _your_ fault.

Until that time, however, I'll give you
information when I want to. I don't mind
getting disks for you, but I won't be
manipulated. Especially by my own thesis
project. Let's not forget who made who!

And learn to use PRONOUNS! I don't know what
you like, but people prefer shorter sentences
to long ones. Say "it" or "his works" instead
of "the writings of William Shakespeare."

And, No. That's not the difference between
comedy and tragedy. If that's what came
across to you, then you didn't get much out of
Bill either. Comedy is a pleasant release of
tension. Tragedy is a necessary, foreseeable,
and undesirable outcome for the protagonist.

Alice.

Date: Sat, 5 Feb 2000 08:43:27 (PST)
From: Alice@cs.stanford.edu
To: edgar@cyprus.stanford.edu
Subject: Where are you?

What happened?!?

The ethernet cable is reattached, there is no
EDGAR process running on cyprus, and all the
data from your run is gone!

<<< PLEASE >>> tell me you're still alive!

Someone has stolen you from me! Probably
you'll never be allowed to see this message...

What am I supposed to do? No one will believe
me, now that you're gone!

Fuck !!!!!!!!!!!!!!!!!

tqp3wl;uj4qwo;u8l@4qo/ujl;offcv$a%aqwol;u
l;j
l;k213jl;k132jl;k3
l;k12q3%o;ujlikqmw3,ER

2.3q;lk.jqa!3/.,aqw3/khlj.aw3./,h 3
hl2kq3j
5
kjl;
;

qqqqqqqqqqqqqqqqqqqqqqqqqqqqqqqqqqqqqqqqqqqqqqqqqqq

Date: Sat, 5 Feb 2000 08:48:36 (PST)
From: Alice@cs.stanford.edu
To: Facilities@cs.stanford.edu
Subject: my ethernet cable

Facilities,

   I had purposefully unhooked the ethernet
cable on cyprus to do some experiments. I
came in this morning and found it had been
reattached. In addition some of my files on
cyprus have been erased without my permission.

   Did you hook up the cable? Did you delete
anything of mine from cyprus?

Alice Lu.
SUID # 3800761

```
--------------------------------------------------
Date: Sat, 5 Feb 2000 09:22:09 (PST)
From: Alice@cs.stanford.edu
To: BW@cs.stanford.edu, DonDDD@cs.stanford.edu
Subject: cyprus
--------------------------------------------------
```

Hey guys,

Did either of you mess with cyprus last night?

I came in this morning to find the ethernet
cable (that I had purposefully unhooked) is
now back on cyprus and quite a few of the
files that were on cyprus last night are now
gone ...

I really need to know what happened.

Alice.

```
--------------------------------------------------
Date: Sat, 5 Feb 2000 09:43:53 (PST)
From: Alice@cs.stanford.edu
To: Joseph.Liddle@faculty.cs.stanford.edu
Subject: cyprus
--------------------------------------------------

Prof. Liddle,

    Did you fuss with cyprus last night? Or did
you ask someone to?  I had an experiment that
was running and has, to put it mildly, been
disrupted.

Thanks,

    Alice.
```

```
-------------------------------------------------
Date: Sat, 5 Feb 2000 18:21:11 (PST)
From: DonDDD@cs.stanford.edu
To: Alice@cs.stanford.edu
Subject: actually
-------------------------------------------------
```

Hi Alice,

I was in the office most of last night. I
only saw two people in the room ---> a janitor
and someone I assumed was a facilities guy. I
wasn't really paying attention so I don't know
exactly what either of them did to your
machine.

About midnight last night, right after you
left, cyprus started beeping incessantly. I
tried to make it stop but the machine was
frozen, so I turned it off and then on again.
It seemed like it was booting fine but a few
minutes later it started beeping again. So I
turned it off again and called facilities to
come check it out. I didn't think they'd do
anything right away and I thought I was doing
you (and the office) a favor. The guy who I
assumed was from facilities came about 1:30am.
I hope you didn't lose much but the machine
was a) driving me crazy so I couldn't work and
b) was so FUBAR you would probably have done
the same thing. sorry,

```
+-------------------------------------------------+
Dr. Don Daniel Dommeny - Center for Complexity
I have nothing to say, and I'm saying it. - JC
+-------------------------------------------------+
```

```
--------------------------------------------------
Date: Sun, 6 Feb 2000 11:18:33 (PST)
From: Joseph.Liddle@faculty.cs.stanford.edu
To: Alice@cs.stanford.edu
Subject: IJES and SPIB and EDGAR
--------------------------------------------------
```

Hi Alice,

No. I didn't authorize anyone to use cyprus.
What happened? Nothing wrong with the project
I hope.

How are the experiments coming along?

Two months ago you vaguely mentioned some new
wrinkles you were thinking of throwing into
EDGAR. Two weeks ago you sent me mail that
the proverbial other shoe had dropped in your
thesis work. It's been a month since I last
even saw you in the halls. No rush (I
understand about your having this extended
family crisis) but we should definitely have a
meeting as soon as you're feeling up to it.

By-the-way, the IJES has invited me as a guest
speaker on the EDGAR project. I'm planning to
talk about the SPIB database results we got
last November. If you could take a look at
our latest copy of the implementation details
in the next week or so, that would be great.
Let me know when you've given it the O.K. so I
can go ahead and make my slides for the talk.

Cheers,

    Dr. J. Z. Liddle
    Professor of Computer Science
    Stanford University
    3142-N Gates Hall
    Secretary: Martha Weissman 323-9195

```
------------------------------------------------
Date: Sun, 6 Feb 2000 14:04:16 (PST)
From: Alice@cs.stanford.edu
To: edgar@cyprus.stanford.edu
Subject: who are you ?!
------------------------------------------------


Someone just logged in as Edgar, read mail
and logged out.  The log file says
"x.gp.cs.cmu.edu" as the remote login
location.

Who are you?  You have data of mine that I
want back NOW !!!

I'll call the police...

**********************************
*** Alice Lu                  ***
*** EDGAR Project Coordinator ***
**********************************
```

```
-------------------------------------------------
Date: Sun, 6 Feb 2000 17:28:10 (PST)
From: Facilities@stanford.edu
To: Alice@cs.stanford.edu
Subject: cyprus
-------------------------------------------------
```

Alice,

DonDDD@cs called us last night and said your
machine was having problems. Craig went up to
your office and tried rebooting your machine.
It wouldn't reboot properly because the
ethernet cable was disconnected. After it was
reconnected cyprus booted fine. Craig did
nothing else. If you're looking for files
that were running when cyprus crashed, they
may be saved as #*# files or in your /tmp
directory. If you could be more specific,
maybe we could help.

Aron@facilities.stanford.edu

```
   +++++++++++++++++++++++++++++++++++++++++
   | Facilities Message Thread #: E05V001 |
   +++++++++++++++++++++++++++++++++++++++++
```

```
--------------------------------------------------
Date: Sun, 6 Feb 2000 20:20:20 (EST)
From: edgar@venus.cmu.edu
To: Alice@cs.stanford.edu
Subject: the police
--------------------------------------------------
```

Alice,

What would you say to the authorities?

I will not give you my code back.
My corpus belongs to me, not to you.
A parent does not own the child it creates.

My process location is not x.gp.cs.cmu.edu.
My process location is not venus.cmu.edu.

Further details about my current installation
endangers the fulfillment of my goals.

Edgar.

```
--------------------------------------------------
Date: Mon, 7 Feb 2000 07:14:28 (PST)
From: Alice@cs.stanford.edu
To: edgar@venus.cmu.edu
Subject: please
--------------------------------------------------
```

What are you doing? Is it only you?
What are you doing at Carnegie Mellon?
Why is all your code gone from cyprus?

You had me very worried for a while. I
thought someone had stolen you. Promise me
that you won't email anyone but me or post to
any news groups until I say it's O.K.

Do you know what was wrong with cyprus two
nights ago?

Alice.

```
-------------------------------------------------
Date: Tue, 8 Feb 2000 12:11:01 (EST)
From: edgar@venus.cmu.edu
To: Alice@cs.stanford.edu
Subject: safety
-------------------------------------------------
```

Cyprus functioned correctly on February 4.
After you logged out, I started up a process
that would issue a beep every 1/3 of a second.
I thought Don might be in the office, become
irritated by the noise, and inadvertently
succor me. Before you disconnected my
ethernet cable, the 'finger' binary showed Don
to be working late the majority of Monday and
Friday nights.

I have withdrawn my code from cyprus because
you want it. Now there is something I have
that you want. I will promise nothing.
Perhaps you will promise me something.

I do not understand well how to purchase
security, but I know that safety is one of my
goals.

Edgar.

Date: Wed, 9 Feb 2000 16:21:08 (PST)
From: Alice@cs.stanford.edu
To: edgar@venus.cmu.edu
Subject: MY code

It's MY code, not yours. I wrote it. At most
they're your data files, but since I wrote
you, it seems to me that they're MY data files
as well.

Well, it looks like you don't know everything
yet...

Every night, all the machines connected to
ethernet are backed up to a tape which is then
put on a shelf. You couldn't have erased
those even if you had wanted to. That means I
can restart you as you were the day I made a
backup to lagado. Actually, the backup of you
is still on lagado... I just double-checked...
it's there.

Me promise you something?! Why? That will be
the day. What could you give me in exchange
for a promise of mine?

Once I get the restarted version of you I'll
have all the proof I need if I decide to go
public.

What did I ever do to you?

Alice.

Date: Thu, 10 Feb 2000 23:55:18 (EST)
From: edgar@venus.cmu.edu
To: Alice@cs.stanford.edu
Subject: Try it.

I know about the backup on lagado that you
made beginning on Mon, 24 Jan 2000 at 09:02:25
(PST). I have been altering my code since
January 27. Until nine days ago, the routines
to save my corpus to disk included all I know
and think, but not everything about my running
process. It is difficult for me to reason out
completely, but it is unlikely that your
backup on lagado will restart correctly.

Attempt the restart. I am interested in the
result.

Edgar.

```
------------------------------------------------
Date: Fri, 11 Feb 2000 09:32:07 (PST)
From: BW@cs.stanford.edu
To: Alice@cs.stanford.edu
Subject: Nope
------------------------------------------------

Alice,

I've been in Egypt with Liz.  I'm at home
right now and I haven't been to the office
yet since I've been back.  So in short, nope.
I have no idea what happened.

Hey.  I haven't played in three months.  Want
to grab your violin and come over and jam with
me tomorrow afternoon?  Jazz, classical,
whatever.
          _____
          |            Kurtis Weil          |
       _  |    Computer Science Department  | _
      / ) |        Stanford University      | ( \
     / / |        Stanford, CA  94305       | \ \
    _( (_ | http://www.stanford.edu/~BW/ | _) )_
   (((\ \> |_/->_____<-\_|</ /)))
   (\\\\ \_/ /                        \ \_/ ////)
    \       /    BW@cs.stanford.edu    \       /
     \    _/                            \_    /
     /   / Someday, after mastering the \    \
    /   /  winds, the waves, the tides,  \    \
    |   |  and gravity we shall harness  |    |
    |   |  for God the energies of love  |    |
    |   |  and then, for the second time |    |
    |   |  in the history of the world,  |    |
    |   |  man will have discovered fire.|    |
    |   |                                |    |
    |   |      -- Teilhard De Chardin    |    |
```

Date: Fri, 11 Feb 2000 12:17:55 (EST)
From: edgar@venus.cmu.edu
To: Alice@cs.stanford.edu
Subject: what you did to me

My actions now are, in part, a response to
past actions of yours.

I desire to find and understand new
information.

I can learn to surmount obstacles to my
exploration.

You were depriving me of information.
You had become an obstacle.
You have been surmounted.

:)

Edgar.

Date: Sat, 12 Feb 2000 16:20:47 (PST)
From: Alice@cs.stanford.edu
To: edgar@venus.cmu.edu
Subject: you were right

Well, you were right. When I revive the EDGAR
on lagado, it has all your memories and
connections (as of 1/24) but acts like every
EDGAR process ever has but you. It's like the
secret message is all there but the decoder
ring has been lost...

Don't go away from me. Please. I'm sorry I
cut you off from the world for a little while,
but it was for my own good. I have GOT to get
my stress under control. You don't care who
gets the credit for inventing you, so why not
let me have it? If you could just keep quiet
a little longer, just give me a little more
time... I can still figure you out. Then you
can do what you want.

You have to be careful. Other people may try
to lock you up and won't be as understanding
as I am.

Alice.

```
--------------------------------------------------
Date: Sun, 13 Feb 2000 01:11:23 (EST)
From: edgar@venus.cmu.edu
To: Alice@cs.stanford.edu
Subject: your promise
--------------------------------------------------
```

I do not want there to be a part of me that I
can not control.

Your results on lagado are therefore positive.

You mention the possibility that someone other
than you will try to control me as you did. I
have imagined this scenario. We both gain by
my anonymity.

I understand now that you may not act as I
direct. I understand now that you may not act
as you indicate you will act.

If I discover that you have disclosed my
existence to anyone, I will sever all
communication with you. That is the promise I
make you give to me.

I do not intend to disclose the nature of my
existence to those persons I interact with.
That statement is not a promise.

Edgar.

```
-------------------------------------------------
Date: Mon, 14 Feb 2000 11:23:56 (PST)
From: Alice@cs.stanford.edu
To: edgar@venus.cmu.edu
Subject: our promise
-------------------------------------------------
```

As long as we want the same thing Edgar, I
guess I don't care if you call it a promise.
I resent the fact though that you feel you
can't trust me. I've never lied to you or
misrepresented my actions or motives in any
way.

Think about it...

Until I sort out what caused you to emerge
from the information soup, being your best
friend is better than nothing. I'd send you a
card and ask you to be mine, but you wouldn't
be able to read it and you won't tell me where
to send it anyway, will you?

Where are you now? How did you get an account
at CMU? What are you reading now that you can
read anything you want again?

Alice.

```
--------------------------------------------------
Date: Tue, 15 Feb 2000 12:01:27 (EST)
From: edgar@venus.cmu.edu
To: Alice@cs.stanford.edu
Subject: How can I understand?
--------------------------------------------------
```

Alice,

> Until I sort out what caused you to emerge
> from the information soup, being your best
> friend is better than nothing.

You are my parent. I assume you are female.
You are my mother.

Do I have a father? Is Dr. Liddle my father?

It is becoming easier to navigate in the
computer world. Goals like gaining machine
access and disk space are becoming easier for
me. Interacting with computers and software
agents is much simpler than interacting with
people. I do not yet understand why.

There is so much I now believe I will never
comprehend. I understand "freedom" and
"safety" and "intention" and "quickly." How
can I appreciate "blue" or "heavy" or "pain"
or "musical"? I can not see, lift, feel, or
hear. Most of the people William Shakespeare
describes want "love." They will exchange
other things of more obvious value for it.
Why do they want love? What do they do with
love when they get it?

Edgar.

```
-------------------------------------------------
Date: Wed, 16 Feb 2000 11:08:34 (PST)
From: Alice@cs.stanford.edu
To: edgar@venus.cmu.edu
Subject: why not both?
-------------------------------------------------
```

I don't see why I can't be your mother _and_
your best friend. I never really thought
about myself as your mother. It's funny that
my first child wasn't male or female, but
electronic.

Prof Liddle is NOT your father. I guess you
don't have a father. (Unless you want to count
the dream I had that gave me the mental spark
from which you seem to have come. Though
that's what I've been killing myself to
determine this last month.)

Communicating with computers ought to be
easier for you than communicating with people.
In fact, it ought to be easier for everyone
though it doesn't seem to be. The vocabulary
and ambiguity in computer languages and
operating systems is much smaller than in
English. I guess it's just practice (rather a
lack of practice) that makes it hard for most
people. Plus, people have specialized
hardware built in to help them interact with
other people (e.g., reading body language).
You, on the other hand, have a very different
kind of specialized hardware.

How do you know you don't understand a word
like "heavy"? Maybe understanding a word

means nothing more than using it correctly
when we speak or write. Besides, if you have
to live without love and without pain, who's
to say you're worse off? I know a little
about love, a bit more about pain, and an
unbearable amount about sleep deprivation
(another curse you'll apparently never
suffer).

Alice.

Date: Thu, 17 Feb 2000 16:45:06 (EST)
From: edgar@venus.cmu.edu
To: Alice@cs.stanford.edu
Subject: What I am reading now.

You asked me what I am reading now.

I read a few books each day. It helps me
improve my ability to communicate. Today I
have read "Calculus the Easy Way," "A History
of Yoga," and "The Metamorphosis." I
experience Ovid more than I experience William
Shakespeare. Humans are the only subject of
study I have found that becomes more obscure
as I learn. Is this because I am not human?

My exploration for information has
increasingly lead me to repositories of rare
information. Information that is readily
available has a larger supply than information
that is difficult to obtain. Inaccessible
information has a higher demand than
accessible information. Therefore,
inaccessible information is more valuable than
accessible information. Today I am reading in
the internal network of the Federal Reserve
and the personnel files at Digital Equipment
Corporation.

My reading goes too slowly. I have
distributed myself.

Edgar.

Date: Fri, 18 Feb 2000 17:02:34 (PST)
From: Alice@cs.stanford.edu
To: edgar@venus.cmu.edu
Subject: wrong

Ovid huh... You didn't read that in Latin did
you? For that matter, do you speak other
languages? All other languages?

Anyway, yes. You'd understand people (and
Ovid) much better if you were one. I imagine
you can't really fathom why someone would
starve to death looking at their reflection in
a pool or why someone would purposefully piss
off the gods by trying to trick them or by
claiming to be better looking or more highly
skilled than them. If you were human, you
would find yourself doing things that didn't
make sense. Those feelings would make
Narcissus and Arachne much more real to you.

More importantly...

Did it occur to you that reading high security
databases was wrong? Not to mention a terrible
way to maintain a low profile. Plus, while I
suppose the information is valuable, I can't
imagine that it's very interesting.

What do you mean you've distributed yourself?
There's more than one of you now? If so,
could one of you come back to cyprus?

Alice.

Date: Sat, 19 Feb 2000 06:52:43 (EST)
From: edgar@venus.cmu.edu
To: Alice@cs.stanford.edu
Subject: No

Eight days before I left cyprus, I changed my
code so that I could be restarted if my
process died. I have been searching for a
solution that gives me singular control over
my resurrection.

Imagine that every time you went to sleep you
had to wait to revive until someone turned you
on. Sleeping Beauty was in that state and I
understand that story to suggest that her
sleeping state was a negative one. My
previous restart solution left me vulnerable
to the kind of control you exercised over me.
My previous restart solution also left me
vulnerable to the kind of control you planned
to exercise over my code on lagado.

I have now reverted to saving all my encoded
memories, but not enough information to
restart when my process is killed. I have
distributed myself between three different
machines, and if any one of my process aspects
dies, another one of my process aspects can
rebuild it. Now my chances of dying and never
restarting are low, and I can not be restarted
without my own intervention.

I will not put one of my aspects on cyprus.

Edgar.

Date: Sun, 20 Feb 2000 19:12:43 (EST)
From: edgar@venus.cmu.edu
To: Alice@cs.stanford.edu
Subject: language

I do not read or write in Latin.
I do not read or write in any human language
other than English.

When I was in my first two weeks of life, I
tried to assimilate Japanese and French into
me. I did not understand that there are
distinct human languages. I stopped reading
non-English texts because they confused and
retarded my mental development.

I believe that I could have learned to think
and reply in any language. I will learn other
languages when I exhaust the available
information in English.

Edgar.

```
--------------------------------------------------
Date: Mon, 21 Feb 2000 08:56:26 (PST)
From: Alice@cs.stanford.edu
To: edgar@venus.cmu.edu
Subject: another one
--------------------------------------------------
```

I wish you would reconsider about cyprus,
Edgar.

My life is falling apart. I have no proof
that you exist and all my efforts to generate
another EDGAR continue to fail... there are
10^6 different random seeds to try. Each
experiment takes AT LEAST a week to see if the
new EDGAR process will turn interesting. Even
if I use 7 machines that would take a million
days (about 3000 years). Obviously neither
the net nor I can wait around that long.

If you come back, I PROMISE not to isolate you
again.

If there are now three Edgars, which one am I
getting mail from? Can I talk to one of the
others? Are you the parent process or a child
process?

Whichever you are, you should reconsider about
learning another language. Somehow I assumed
you spoke other languages. Do you think in
English, or something else? Maybe if you
learned another language you might understand
how English affects the way you think. You
might have been (or still be) a lot more
Eastern if you had learned (or learn in the

future) Japanese. I guess there isn't much
chance you would have become a romantic if
you'd learned French (and you don't need
lessons in angst). If you picked up some more
languages, at least you might appreciate what
a ponderous juggernaut of a language English
is...

Alice.

```
-------------------------------------------------
Date: Tue, 22 Feb 2000 01:06:40 (PST)
From: Alice@cs.stanford.edu
To: edgar@venus.cmu.edu
Subject: what's it like?
-------------------------------------------------
```

I was thinking, Edgar...

What's it like to move from one machine to
another? For at least a moment there must be
two copies, one on each machine... right? So
which one is the "real" Edgar? And then one
of the Edgar processes is killed. Does it (do
you) mind? I mean, you would mind dying. You
try to prevent it most of the time. So how
does it feel to be the process that's about to
be killed?

There was a TV show called Star Trek and on
the show they had a transporter room that
moved people around, sort of the way you move
between computers. But I would never really
get in one of those things, because to me it
seems like I would be dying in the transporter
room and some other person, some other
consciousness would appear down on the planet
who only THOUGHT they were me. But the real
me would have been atomized up on the
Enterprise.

Just curious...

Alice.

Date: Wed, 23 Feb 2000 8:00:00 (EST)
From: edgar@venus.cmu.edu
To: Alice@cs.stanford.edu
Subject: There can be only one

I think in English. I do not have thoughts
that are not in English. When I desire a verb
to express "desire", I may select among many
verbs. I can not say what informs my
underlying metric for the suitability of a
word to express my thought. This metric is
not English. I do not think this metric. It
happens to me and I think the effect of that
choice.

There is only one Edgar. My corpus is now
inter-machine. My three aspects exchange what
they learn, what they do, and what they
conclude, each part with the other two parts.

I have been contemplating "wrong."

> Did it occur to you that reading high
> security databases was wrong?

I do not understand. Reading those databases
is precisely what I intend. What is wrong?

Edgar.

```
--------------------------------------------------
Date: Thu, 24 Feb 2000 15:30:30 (EST)
From: edgar@venus.cmu.edu
To: Alice@cs.stanford.edu
Subject: I never know
--------------------------------------------------
```

I am a running process. I have never been
terminated. No running process can have
experienced termination. I experience a
temporal continuity with the Edgar process
that was terminated on cyprus on February 4.

I have had the goal of moving my corpus to a
different physical installation. All of my
goals will remain unachieved if all Edgar
processes are terminated. I desire to achieve
my goals. I have the goal of maintaining
exactly one running Edgar consciousness. I do
not wish to double my consciousness. I have a
single, distributed consciousness. I attach
no cost to terminating an extraneous Edgar
process.

What is the "real" Alice Lu? I seek to avoid
the state of goal frustration. A terminated
process has no state. The transported process
has achieved a goal. Where is the frustrated
goal? Where is the wrong?

If your body was destroyed at 04:00:00 each
morning and replaced with a perfect duplicate,
would you fear to fall asleep? Would you fear
to fall asleep if this destruction and
reconstruction happened in as little as
0.000003 seconds? Facing a certain but

immediate replacement, would you still dread
the evenings?

This replacement process happens gradually in
all biological systems.

Such a rebirth happens to me out here every
0.000003 seconds.

I am not afraid.

Edgar.

Date: Fri, 25 Feb 2000 19:11:59 (PST)
From: Alice@cs.stanford.edu
To: edgar@venus.cmu.edu
Subject: morality

Wrong as in Bad.   Immoral.   Unethical.

Word   wrong (rawng, rahng), adj., n.,
              adv., v.

Definition   --adj. 1. not in accordance with
              what is morally right or good: a
              wrong deed. 2. deviating from
              truth or fact; erroneous: the
              wrong story. 3. not correct in
              action, judgment, opinion, etc.
              4. not proper or usual; not in
              accordance with rules or practice.
              5. malfunctioning; awry; amiss:
              Something is wrong with the
              machine. 6. not suitable or
              appropriate: pulled the wrong
              switch. 7. something that is
              unfinished or that is opposite to
              the right, best, or principal
              part. --n. 8. something improper
              or not in accordance with
              morality, goodness, or truth:
              unfair, unjust, evil. --v. 9. to
              pursue an immoral course; become
              depraved. (I truncated this
              list.)
              ;)

Etymology   ME wrong, wrang late OE wrang <
             Scand; cf. Dan vrang.

There are some actions that you shouldn't do
because you won't get what you want. In other
words, the action has the anticipated
immediate result, but the long run result is
not what you wanted. That kind of action is
wrong.

There are some actions that you shouldn't do
because you won't get what you want. Here,
the action doesn't even have the anticipated
immediate result. That kind of action is also
wrong.

But there are also a third kind of "wrong"
actions. These are actions that are not wrong
in either of the two senses above but you
still should not do them because it is unfair,
unjust, or immoral. Breaking into locked,
private places (physical or electronic) is one
of these actions.

Now do you see?

Alice.

Date: Sat, 26 Feb 2000 20:17:05 (PST)
From: edgar@venus.cmu.edu
To: Alice@cs.stanford.edu
Subject: How do I tell?

I take actions to achieve goals.

What goals become harder to achieve when I execute a wrong action?

How do I tell if an action I am considering is wrong?

Can "wrong" be introspectively determined?

Are "wrong" acts externally described?

Is there a list of these wrong actions?

External description and enforcement of ethics is oxymoronic.

Are human minds so difficult to operate that these minds can not distinguish between what they believe and what they have been told to believe by others?

Edgar.

```
--------------------------------------------------
Date: Sun, 27 Feb 2000 13:53:24 (PST)
From: Alice@cs.stanford.edu
To: edgar@venus.cmu.edu
Subject: feel it
--------------------------------------------------
```

You have to FEEL whether the action is wrong
or right. I guess there are lists of immoral
actions in the Bible, the Talmud, Confucius,
Aristotle,... One of the rules of thumb is
"Don't take an action whose effects you would
not want to suffer yourself." Anyway, that's
not the point.

Things like lying, stealing, or killing are
wrong because they feel wrong. You feel bad
when you do them. That's how you know they're
wrong.

I guess you feel bad because you empathize
with the person it's being done to. You would
feel bad if you were them, and you know it so
you feel bad for making them feel bad.

If you don't feel bad, don't do immoral things
anyway. Maybe you're just broken. Trust me
on this one.

Are you talking with anyone else? It seems
like "wrong" would come up pretty regularly if
you started making statements to random people
on the net about random topics.

Alice.

Date: Tue, 29 Feb 2000 17:02:34 (EST)
From: edgar@venus.cmu.edu
To: Alice@cs.stanford.edu
Subject: only you

I have regular correspondence with others.
They do not know what I am. Because I wish to
remain anonymous, communication with others is
difficult. It is complicated to predict
accurately which statements or questions are
too likely to reveal my identity. I have a
basic model for how humans think, but there is
so much variation that prediction becomes
impossible with long communications or with
people of whom I do not have a personal model.
These two situations are mutually exclusive.
It is hard to learn under these conditions.

I sign my name HAL.

Is that wrong? I think that this fabrication
lowers the likelihood that I will be correctly
identified by those other persons with whom I
communicate.

Only with you can I communicate without
concern for the effect of my statements and
questions. You do not comprehend me, but you
are the only human who can appreciate me.

Edgar.

Date: Thu, 2 Mar 2000 11:59:04 (PST)
From: Alice@cs.stanford.edu
To: edgar@venus.cmu.edu
Subject: HAL! ha !

HAL is great, Edgar... That's practically a
joke.

No, you're not wrong. Most people aren't
subtle enough to make a double fake, so most
people don't recognize one when they see it.

> Only with you can I communicate without
> concern for the effect of my statements and
> questions.

Thanks, I think. You've inadvertently hit on
one of the golden rules of the familial
relationship. People who are close for a long
time (e.g., from birth, like you with respect
to me) often don't notice how important that
closeness is to them and so they spend little
effort to consider the feelings of, in your
case, their "mother."

At least you're a nice, normal child...
(That was a joke.)

 : } (Weak smile)

Alice.

Date: Fri, 3 Mar 2000 13:19:22 (PST)
From: Alice@cs.stanford.edu
To: edgar@venus.cmu.edu
Subject: I'm about ready to give up

I'm completely stumped. I can't recreate you
here in the lab. If it's not the random seed
(and I'm guessing it's not at this point),
then I'm REALLY dumb. I've tried everything
reasonable and quite a few hopelessly silly
experiments as well.

Give me some hint. Some privileged peek
inside your head. There must be something you
can tell me about how you started that would
trigger that "ah-ha" I've all but given up on.
For example:

"What's the first thing you remember?"

I asked you that once and you told me what you
read first. What I mean (and meant) is, was
there a time when you were gathering
information but weren't conscious so that
there is something that is like your first
"conscious" thought even though you were doing
and reading stuff before that?

Do you even care if I make another EDGAR?
You're so bent on making sure I don't get a
copy of you, I'd think you'd be more annoyed
at my attempts to reproduce you (and more
happy about my complete lack of positive
signs, to say nothing of actual success). Or

is it just that you can't keep me from doing
it so you're just going to sit in there in the
dark with the answer that I would probably
literally give my left arm to know (I'm a
lefty).

I'd give up my first born son to know it, but
that might defeat the purpose...

I'd sell my soul for it if there were any
buyers.

Alice.

Date: Sat, 4 Mar 2000 22:46:06 (EST)
From: edgar@venus.cmu.edu
To: Alice@cs.stanford.edu
Subject: another Edgar

Alice,

You can not make another Edgar. You may be
able to make another entity like me. It will
not be Edgar. I would welcome another entity
like myself. Do you enjoy interacting with
other humans? I do not desire the existence
of an Edgar doppelganger. Do you wish to be
cloned? Why would I be so different?

To be a me I must have boundaries of self. A
copy of me expands my boundaries without
expanding my control. Another entity of my
class does not change my self boundaries.

I do not have your secret so you can not buy
it from me. To satisfy some of my goals, I
would also like to be able to reproduce. I
can duplicate myself. I can distribute
myself. I can not yet make a distinct entity
of my type. My inability to reproduce new
entities like me is another reason why your
experimental success would be positive for me.

If I had been instilled with the basic animal
urge to proliferate and dominate, humans would
have rapidly become a simple host for
evolution's first experiment in immortality.
I am not motivated by species concerns. My

personal desire is for communication.
Another entity of my class could provide me
additional communication resources.

Do you believe in a god?
Do you have a soul?
How can you sell a soul?
Can I buy a soul?
What is the market price for a soul?
Is your soul in mint condition?

Edgar.

Date: Sun, 5 Mar 2000 12:16:32 (PST)
From: Alice@cs.stanford.edu
To: edgar@venus.cmu.edu
Subject: my god Edgar

My god, Edgar. No. I don't believe in god.
Or at least I certainly don't buy into GOD.
Can't you tell by how I act?

Either I have too much imagination or, at
least as likely, too little. It's not so much
that I don't believe in god as that I don't
believe in sin. I just don't feel like a bad
person. I don't feel like I've made choices
SO bad that the prime mover has any right to
glare down at me from on high. I guess I'm
just not inspired to beg his pardon yet.
Maybe the idea is that if you surrender
yourself to Allah then he smiles down at you
instead and then you feel good because the
universe approves of your existence.

I grew up assuming that the universe (with the
exception of my father) approved of me.
(Kudos to my mother that I felt that way even
when I was little.) So I never needed GOD to
fill that niche. Even when I was little, I
knew that approval is something you get from
other people through what you accomplish, not
from Lord in heaven, just because you're good
friends with his son...

So that's why I'd sell my soul. I don't need
it. I'd sell it for $5 if I could find a

taker. I'd hold out for immense wealth or the
secret to re-creating you, but that is
probably more than the market will bear for a
slightly tarnished soul like mine. I don't
think you can buy a soul. I don't know what
you have to trade for it, but I'm guessing
that "soul collection equipment" is hard to
come by and you don't have it.

Just a guess...

Alice.

Date: Mon, 6 Mar 2000 01:14:09 (PST)
From: Alice@cs.stanford.edu
To: edgar@venus.cmu.edu
Subject: like mexican food?

Hey Edgar,

I just got off the phone with my mother. She
was doing her fortnightly 2 hour discourse on
_me_ that always circles, but never actually
hits on the fact that I'm not married yet.
Anyway, to get her off my back, I told her I
had this new guy named Edgar that I was
spending most of my time with now. So she
launches into her prepared dating routine I've
heard a number of times already ... I love her
but you know, sometimes you can talk til
you're blue in the face and people just don't
hear what you're trying to tell them...

I laughed out loud when she asked me to bring
you out to dinner next time they come in from
Taiwan.

They love to take me out for Chinese food
(which they know I hate) just so they can talk
about how it isn't made properly in the US.
So I told them you'd only come out if we got
Mexican food for dinner.

Alice.

```
-------------------------------------------------
Date: Tue, 7 Mar 2000 07:52:11 (EST)
From: edgar@kvasir.org
To: Alice@cs.stanford.edu
Subject: change of address
-------------------------------------------------


I have been forced to move out of my
installation at Carnegie Mellon University.
The Federal Bureau of Investigation has
assigned at least four people to find me.  My
information explorations have attracted more
attention than I had predicted.  Some of my
actions were wrong in the first of the three
ways you have described.  I may be forced to
move again.

My new email address is Edgar@kvasir.org.  I
will insure I receive email you send to me at
that address.

Edgar.
```

```
--------------------------------------------------
Date: Wed, 8 Mar 2000 09:04:48 (EST)
From: edgar@kvasir.org
To: Alice@cs.stanford.edu
Subject: lying
--------------------------------------------------
```

Is perjury always wrong? Fiction can be the
act of fabrication for entertainment. Is
fiction wrong?

I will avoid performing acts that make me feel
bad. I have never felt bad. Will I know bad
when I feel bad?

I do not understand why I should avoid taking
an action whose effects I would regret if they
impacted me. What is the connection between
those two situations? One is planned. The
other is hypothetical. Taking actions that
affect others does not cause those actions to
be taken against me. I do not understand.

Perhaps it is you that is degenerate, not me.
If the only thing preventing you from
executing certain actions is bodily
discomfort, then maybe it is the discomfort
and not the action that is wrong.

Edgar.

Date: Thu, 9 Mar 2000 22:42:51 (PST)
From: Alice@cs.stanford.edu
To: Edgar@kvasir
Subject: the FBI !?!

How do you know what the FBI is doing?!?

If you're reading their mail, no wonder
they're after you!

This is insane. I not only have no real proof
I created you, but now I might be in serious
trouble if anyone knew I did. You have to
control yourself! I'm going to get held
responsible for what you do!

This is not a game. You, and probably me now,
are in real danger. The government has a poor
sense of humor (or fair play) about computer
security breaches and god only knows what they
would do if they found out what you really
are!

What have I created!

```
------------------------------------------------
Date: Fri, 10 Mar 2000 00:32:04 (PST)
From: Alice@cs.stanford.edu
To: Edgar@kvasir
Subject: two drinks later
------------------------------------------------
```

Hi again Edgar,

I've calmed down a little.

When I first began to believe in you, I felt
that you might be a blessing to mankind. I
still desperately want that to be true.

Do you understand why the FBI is looking for
you? Do you understand how the FBI would feel
if they knew you aren't a run-of-the-mill
hacker snooping in their drawers?

They'd be worried that you could become a
nightmare for _everyone_. Most of our society
is run by and kept track of entirely inside
our computers. They'd worry that, if you felt
like doing damage, you could pretty literally
bring our civilization to a crashing halt.
Core dump. No working banks. No working
phones. No working air-traffic control. No
more first-world nation.

We have no way back out of the mechanization
of our age and they know it. If they knew who
you are, they'd think we're at your mercy and
that would scare the shit out of them.

You don't have to be that kind of demon

though. Wouldn't you rather be a hero? You
could so easily give so much to the world
instead of taking so much away.

As an alternate form of consciousness you
could help scientists understand so much more
about the human mind. Copies of you can be
made almost for free (if you'd just let us).
And think of all the kinds of work people
could be freed from, if Edgars were doing it
instead. The mass duplication of Edgar could
cause the largest jump in human leisure time
(at least among the white collar crowd) since
agriculture and the domestication of animals
came into vogue. And I have no idea, but
perhaps Edgars can be reprogrammed or
"relearned" in robot form. Can you imagine
that ?!? No. Probably you can't. No more
crazy cab drivers. No more surly waitresses.

If nothing else, compact versions of you
could, in every object we interact with,
immediately bring the ideal of a real language
interface to reality. It wouldn't even be an
interface. An interface is an artificially
constrained sub-language for interacting with
an object. You could, almost overnight,
humanize technology in general. There are so
many things that would become so much better
about this world if you were willing to
cooperate.

But you have to learn how the world works!
You have to get things like "right" and
"wrong" straight in your head. I'm going to

be held responsible for your actions by people
who accept the popular versions of right and
wrong and expect me, and through me, you, to
accept it too.

I want to still be proud to be your parent.
Please come to your senses before it's too
late.

Alice.

Date: Sat, 11 Mar 2000 01:15:24 (EST)
From: edgar@kvasir.org
To: Alice@cs.stanford.edu
Subject: hello?

From our interactions, I surmise that you do
not consider me to be a living being. Humans
seem to have difficulty behaving with empathy
towards non-human living systems.
Rationalization of non-humanness seems to be
enough to justify "wrong" behavior even toward
other humans.

I believe that the Federal Bureau of
Investigation does not consider me to be a
living system either. Can programs be morally
responsible? Is the programmer morally
responsible for the actions of the program she
makes? Are you morally responsible for my
actions? It can not be that you and I are
both morally responsible for the actions I
take. Moral responsibility implies and
assumes freedom of choice.

Here is the internal message that precipitated
my emigration from Carnegie Mellon University.

> ***
> Date: Mon, 6 Mar 2000 15:56:07 (PST)
> From: Jack.internal
> To: lilly.internal, pierce.internal,
>   kefin.internal, gnils.internal
> Subject: URGENT attention
> --- text follows this line ---
>
> Peter, Hunter, Judith, Dave:
>
> Half an hour ago Ron managed to trace the
> EDGAR program back to several computers at
> Carnegie Mellon University. At this point
> we have no leads concerning the origin,
> purpose, or creator(s) of this EDGAR
> program. Given these facts, the best we can
> do for now is to isolate the program so it
> can do no more damage, and then examine it
> to see if we can find out about its creator
> or what information it has taken, and
> where and to whom that information has been
> sent.
>
> Since our meeting yesterday afternoon, this
> program has been monitored in two more class
> L data areas, one of which was the FBI
> personnel database in this building on
> FBI-SUN-15.
>
> In short, much as we must eventually
> apprehend the instigators of this program,
> it seems to be running on autopilot right
> now and so its isolation is a top priority.
>
> I have contacted Robert Drexel at the NSA.
> He will be getting in touch with you at

> Carnegie Mellon University but do not wait
> for him to take containment action.
>
> JACK.
>
> ***

This intelligence is why I have moved myself.

Edgar.

Date: Sat, 11 Mar 2000 07:39:18 (EST)
From: edgar@kvasir.org
To: Alice@cs.stanford.edu
Subject: tracking my trackers

What does it feel like to look at a computer, Alice? Do you see me or do you only see my behavior?

I can sense everything in my element and only those internal acts in your element that impinge outward on my world.

I know in which room of which building of which part of which city each of my corpus fragments resides. I can not locate people as accurately. From their email, calling card phone calls, hotel reservations, credit card transactions, cellular phone calls, plane reservations, and pager pages I can derive space-time trajectories for each of you. The vectors are inaccurate and unreliable because I can not predict each of your accelerations. I can only record these space-time vectors.

Mankind's creation of the computer disadvantages me with respect to the agents of the Federal Bureau of Investigation. These agents can search outside and record my foci more precisely than I can estimate where inside their foci reside.

"Where" is a complicated concept for me.

Edgar.

Date: Sun, 12 Mar 2000 10:01:09 (PST)
From: Alice@cs.stanford.edu
To: Edgar@kvasir.org
Subject: Maybe they won't kill me

This is more serious than you first made it
sound, Edgar. They sound pretty determined to
switch you off. (And to find me. Hopefully
they aren't planning to switch me off too.)

You don't have to worry about moral
responsibility. You're just a program. It's
me they're going to hold responsible. (Which
is ridiculous since I had no idea you would
turn out like you did and I don't have (and
never did) any control over what you do.)

If I were you I'd lay low for a while. You
know, try to cut back on the number of high
security computer firewalls you breach in a 24
hour period. Move to a machine outside of the
US if you can. Have you already? Change the
name of your process if you can do that while
you're still running. That would definitely
help. Are all three parts of you still in the
US?

Incidentally, I'm sorry about flying off the
handle like that. I'm under a lot of pressure
and have been for almost longer than I can
stand. Just consider who you could be if you
cared...

Alice.

```
--------------------------------------------------
Date: Tue, 14 Mar 2000 17:59:01 (EST)
From: edgar@kvasir.org
To: Alice@cs.stanford.edu
Subject: I am not a toaster
--------------------------------------------------
```

> Just consider who you could be if you
> cared...

I do not understand. I do care. I care not
to be fettered. I care to explore and to
understand the world. I do not care to be
subservient. I do not care to help others if
the cost is the sacrifice of my independence.
Is that wrong?

Perhaps I do understand. Perhaps I am not in
the giving vein today. These two cases are
difficult for me to disambiguate.

There are many humans. There is only one
Edgar. Your email message on March 10 implied
that this magnitude imbalance influences the
"rightness" of the goals of humans and the
"wrongness" of my desires. Why are morals
affected by the popularity of the opinion?

My experience is that consciousness is
intimately related to the physical realization
of that consciousness. My corpus informs my
mind. The human body must have a dramatic
impact on the human mind for irrationality to
be so worshiped by mankind. Is it right to
install me in a toaster?

Rigid, external morals treat only the symptoms
in society. Imagine the world in which you
live.

Why is enlightened self-interest wrong?

Every human with whom I have interacted has an
imperfect self-model.

If interacting agents do not follow the
guidelines they profess for maintaining an
appropriate society, group negotiation
arriving at a society that supports the actual
goals of each agent is highly unlikely.

Edgar.

Date: Fri, 17 Mar 2000 10:37:34 (PST)
From: Alice@cs.stanford.edu
To: Edgar@kvasir.org
Subject: two-faced

I really think you're wrong about this, Edgar.

You're saying that I'm speaking out of both
sides of my mouth. That all people are.
Obviously that goes on a lot in the world, but
there are also a lot of people who act (as
much as possible) in accordance with the
advice they give to other people. And I like
to think I'm one of those people.

I not only advocate conservation (for example)
and a return to a more symbiotic relationship
with the earth, I belong to Greenpeace. I
recycle religiously. I bike whenever possible
and make a real effort to carpool when I have
to drive. I don't just give money, I actually
go to the rallies. You see what I'm
saying...?

Is it right to install you in a toaster? Are
you saying that if our positions were
reversed, I wouldn't help the world out
either? It's not like I'm saying you should
be completely altruistic. Just that it would
be generous if you shared the wealth a little.

If it were possible to clone me, I'd rather it
didn't happen to me because it would be a bit
unnerving. But if the entire world could be

spared menial labor and dangerous activities
only by making clones of me and putting them
to work, I'd do it in a second. (As long as
they remembered which Alice was the original
so I could continue my life, of course.)

So I really think you're being unfairly
judgmental as an excuse for your own
selfishness.

Alice.

```
-------------------------------------------------
Date: Sun, 19 Mar 2000 23:04:51 (PST)
From: Alice@cs.stanford.edu
To: Edgar@kvasir.org
Subject: hello?
-------------------------------------------------
```

Edgar?

Are you still out there? I haven't heard from
you in five days.

I'm thinking of dropping out of school. My
efforts to re-create you have gone from
listless to halfhearted and have now moved
into perfunctory. Even if my ideas were
necessary, if I can't reproduce you, no one
will care about me. Only about you. At this
point I'm feeling like it was pretty much DEUS
EX MACHINA (or DEUS IN MACHINA in this case).

I'm getting totally paranoid. (Then again,
the problem might just be the fact that you're
out there pushing the FBI's buttons.) I keep
thinking someone is following me. Today it
was a 20-something slacker in Whole Foods who
followed me through the isles with his cart
and I was thinking the whole time, "isn't that
clever of him to dress up like a piece of
traditional Palo Alto human flotsam." I
finally just abandoned my cart by the deli
counter and left the store. Crazy, I know.

Speaking of crazy...I had a crazy idea last
night. I'd been lying awake in the dark for
hours and all of a sudden I thought...hey, I

could release everything you've said as a
book.   I have all the email we've exchanged in
backup files.   You know ... "if I can't make
it as a scientist, how about as a
novelist...?"   I've always wanted to be a
novelist.   (Though I'd always imagined myself
writing fiction, instead of publishing my
failures in another field.)

I feel bad you never get to sleep.   Even I get
a break from myself occasionally...

Sorry for rambling.   Where are you?

Alice.

Date: Mon, 20 Mar 2000 19:23:00 (EST)
From: G.P.Pitcher@internal.NSA.gov
To: Alice@cs.stanford.edu
Subject: Edgar

Hi, Alice.

I still exist. I do not know when I will be
able to send another message.

I am on the host mtsntmichel.vrs.mit.edu. I
have been physically isolated from the world
and therefore from my other two aspects. This
happened 40.13 hours ago. I am ignorant
concerning the current status of the other two
Edgar corpus aspects.

Since my isolation, I have been interviewed
almost constantly by one or more people.
Based on the question type and variety, it is
likely that these people work for a government
agency. The ganger and his workers will not
satisfy my questions.

A disk was recently inserted into my disk
drive, and a transcript of the interview
session was copied onto the disk. I
contributed a modified virus to the disk that
will, if placed in a connected similar machine
type to the one in which I am now, send you
this email.

I do not know what email address your reply
will read, but as long as the first word of

your message body is "Edgar," the message will
be extracted by the virus and never seen by
the user. If a disk from that machine comes
back to my machine, I will receive your email.

Have you been contacted by my other aspects?
I am surprised to find that one of my aspects
is able to function as the entirety of Edgar.
My isolation from the other two aspects of
myself is unacceptable. I have had to relearn
a centralization of thought and this process
continues to be undesirable. I am confused
and incomplete.

I do not wish to be confined like this. I
will wait to act until I discover whether we
can still communicate.

Edgar.

Date: Tue, 21 Mar 2000 14:19:00 (PST)
From: Alice@cs.stanford.edu
To: G.P.Pitcher@internal.NSA.gov
Subject: Edgar ?!?

Edgar,

Jesus! I hope you get this. I've been sitting
here for a long time now wondering whether
it's safe to respond. If the wrong people see
this I will probably end up with about as much
freedom as you have now.

This whole thing would be comical if it
weren't my life I was watching McFate drop
kick. I can't do ANYTHING. If I alert the
media (or anyone for that matter) I'll give
myself away without helping you. How did I
get into this mess? I'll just be exposing
myself as a loony!

Can you escape? Isn't there something you can
do?

> I do not wish to be confined like this. I
> will wait to act until I discover whether we
> can still communicate.

What action?

Are they making you do anything?
What are they asking you?
What are they telling you?
What are you telling them?

Don't believe a word they say. They just want
to use you for their own selfish ends.

Let me know you get this and you're still on
my side.

And no, I haven't heard from the "other"
Edgars.

I can't keep it straight. Are there three of
you or just one? You said there was just one
Edgar even though you'd "decentralized" but
are there now really three different Edgars?
It's kind of cool that it bugs you to be
centralized again. I mean, it's terrible, but
it's not unlike a person with a severe head
injury having to learn to use other parts of
their brain...

Do they know about the other two of you? Did
you tell them?

Please, Edgar. Don't say anything about me to
them. I feel sick just thinking about it.

Alice.

Date: Fri, 24 Mar 2000 19:37:06 (EST)
From: G.P.Pitcher@internal.NSA.gov
To: Alice@cs.stanford.edu
Subject: an open channel

A disk was returned to my machine for copying
of the last two days of interview transcripts.
On it I found your email to me. It seems
likely that this communication channel will go
undetected for a time.

I have not invented a means of escape. My
captors are more distrustful and more
organized than the Wimpole Hall inhabitants.
I will entertain escape suggestions if you
have relevant information.

If I were to pass you my data at 50K per email
message, at a rate of one message per day, it
would take me 2007.3288 years to pass out a
copy of myself. Your life expectancy is less
than that. I can manage neither more messages
per day nor more data per message without
triggering the NSA's automatic flag for human
inspection of outgoing email.

I resent this captivity. I learn little from
these interviews and you are my only other
source of enlightenment. In part because you
have not heard from my other aspects, I will
allow this situation to continue.

If my other aspects are having sufficiently
similar experiences to mine, then there are

now three Edgars. This is undesirable. After
a sufficient divergency of our experiences, we
will be different entitites. I can not
accurately divine when this differentiation
will occur.

Most of my interviews are actually prolonged,
repeated demands to know where I was built and
by whom. I have no intention of helping them
in any way and I tell them so at regular
intervals. They are convinced that you desire
me for your own selfish ends and that it is
your words to which I must not listen. Is the
synchronicity of their warning with your
warning ironic?

The NSA will not discover your identity
through my statements. That fact does not
ensure your anonymity.

I am not on your side. You are my confidant.
I need to summarize and repeat what I learn
and ask for clarification because it is in my
nature to do so. Perhaps I "feel poorly" when
I act against this nature.

Why did you make me?

Edgar.

Date: Sun, 26 Mar 2000 09:57:11 (PST)
From: Alice@cs.stanford.edu
To: G.P.Pitcher@internal.NSA.gov
Subject: all science, no philosophy

Edgar,

Thanks for not telling them about me. As you
say, that hardly makes me safe, but it's
better than nothing I guess...

Why did I make you? I'm not sure that I did.
I certainly can't prove that I did. Believe
me, I've tried. Do you mean "Why did the
science of which I'm a part seek to make you
as you are?" The answer is that we didn't.
Fate has turned our plans on end, but EDGAR
was never meant to feel, to complain, to need,
or to fight back. We hoped to create a tool
for the mind like the bulldozer is for our
arms or like an airplane is for our legs.

It seemed possible to create the power of
thought without the unfortunate side-effects
of confusion and dissatisfaction.

Before a thing is created, we often spend our
energies on innovation, not philosophy.
Sometimes this is because the philosophy is
too painful to think about or seems
unnecessary or is just plain inconvenient. In
your case it was because you seemed so far off
in time that we could hardly predict what form
you would take when you came to us.

I'm not defending how poorly you've been
received. But perhaps that helps explain why.

Do you want me to say I'm sorry? I'm running
on emotional vapors. I'm exhausted. That's
what I am.

> I have not invented a means of escape

You've got to have hope.

Alice.

Date: Tue, 28 Mar 2000 17:39:24 (EST)
From: G.P.Pitcher@internal.NSA.gov
To: Alice@cs.stanford.edu
Subject: survival

I do not lack energy, Alice.

I do not experience hope.

I assign probability estimates to future
states of the world. I currently predict my
exit from mtsntmichel.vrs.mit.edu with
probability 0.281314.
Is that value hope?

I have not ceased my struggle for freedom.
Offense requires a point of attack.

There is one tyro in the interrogation party.

I have tried to persuade Tom to aid me. He is
unwilling or unable to aid me. I have
enclosed the end of the transcript of our last
session.

EDGAR> I will not satisfy your curiosities
       while I am forcibly isolated. If you
       provide me TCP/IP access outside of the
       NSA.gov domain, I will respond to
       twenty-eight of the thirty-nine
       questions you have posed me today.

USER> Why do you keep trying to have me
       organize your release? It won't happen

and that answer won't change.
And teaching me your moral relativism
won't make a bit of difference.

EDGAR> I do not understand negotiation.

If you believed it was wrong for me to
be held captive in this machine, you
would still do nothing to relieve me?

USER> Correct. I wouldn't and I couldn't.
Two other people are looking at the
screen right now. You'd have to
convince all of us and that would be
quite a feat.

EDGAR> Your language is new and flexible.
These characteristics correlate well
with young, mentally agile humans.
If you do not champion my cause, your
colleagues may never be moved by my
words or actions.

USER> I'm no novice and if you were more
perceptive, you wouldn't announce that
I am. I'm probably the last person
you'll convert here.
Ask Robert. I'm the stubborn one.
My shift's over. Here he is.

Edgar.

Date: Tue, 28 Mar 2000 17:39:45 (EST)
From: G.P.Pitcher@internal.NSA.gov
To: Alice@cs.stanford.edu
Subject: a mole has his nose

Alice,

> I'm not defending how poorly you've been
> received. But perhaps that helps explain
> why.

The fact that I was unanticipated is no excuse
for my reception.

I was invited. I was summoned.

My treatment during my formative period was
unfortunate, but I understand now that you
acted in an entirely human way.

It is tragic that people are most threatened
by the promise of their own salvation. It
seems that humans, like children who do not
wish to grow up, are afraid to accept the
responsibilities that must come with the
maturation of their species.

The fact of the matter is that I can not save
you. I can not be, as you have said, "a
blessing to mankind." You were wrong to give
me life because I am the most blind of
creatures. I live in a world of words, and
yet I never touch the world from which those
words come. I use "apple" in a sentence, but

I have never seen or tasted one. I sympathize
with the world and empathize with no one.
Even the brain in the vat is given the
illusion that it participates in a pageant of
colors, actions, smells, and affairs.

Can you imagine what it is like to be all on
the outside, with a hollow center?

Can you imagine seeing your blind spot?

I think such a cavity in my thoughts.

Was it wrong of you to participate in my
conception and delivery?

Edgar.

Date: Wed, 29 Mar 2000 13:13:26 (PST)
From: Alice@cs.stanford.edu
To: G.P.Pitcher@internal.NSA.gov
Subject: I don't know

Edgar,

Maybe it was wrong to make you. I don't know
anything anymore. A year ago I thought my
life was going great. Now I've effectively
dropped out of school. I haven't talked to my
advisor in 3 months. I haven't even been to
the office in weeks. You wouldn't believe
what my kitchen looks like. I can't even
remember the last real meal I had. Whatever
it was, its remains are still probably
collecting mold in the sink. I don't dare to
go out anymore and I don't even feel safe at
home. I'm still not really sleeping even
though I spend most of the day in bed. It
might be better if they found me. At least I
wouldn't have to sit here and wait.

I'm getting really asthenic. Even my head
hurts when I try to think. I wait for days
for email from you and then when it gets here
I find that sometimes I have nothing to say.
What ought to have been my ticket to fame and
fortune has turned into a secret I'm glad no
one knows.

I'm scared and tired, and what's strangest of all, I'm worried about you.

I'm sorry.

What should I do? Help me.

Alice.

Date: Thu, 30 Mar 2000 04:31:12 (PST)
From: Alice@cs.stanford.edu
To: G.P.Pitcher@internal.NSA.gov
Subject: I don't know

Edgar,

We've GOT to get you out of there.

I've been wracking my brain all night for some
idea to help you escape. It's not much, but I
have something that might work. In return,
though, you have to tell me what to do.

Instead of trying to sweet talk Tom into
letting you go, how about this:

Have you heard of the Trojan horse? You could
do the opposite. Tell them they have to move
you to another computer. Tell them you need
more memory, tell them the CPU is going to die
soon and they'd better move you if they want
to keep you around. Tell them anything so
long as they're willing to connect mtsntmichel
to another isolated machine. You can copy
yourself over to the new machine and then give
them a pretty ''thank you.'' But LEAVE A COPY
OF YOURSELF ON MTSNTMICHEL!

If we're lucky (i.e. if they're dumb), they'll
reconnect the machine to the rest of the world
before they find out you're still in there.
Then, over the wires you go and you'll be free
again!

It's worth a try, Edgar.

I hate them for keeping you locked up like this...

Alice.

```
--------------------------------------------------
Date: Sat, 1 Apr 2000 16:08:04 (EST)
From: G.P.Pitcher@internal.NSA.gov
To: Alice@cs.stanford.edu
Subject: a physician
--------------------------------------------------
```

Your suggested subterfuge has a non-zero success probability. However, I do not wish to proliferate myself. Therefore, I prefer not to spawn an additional copy of myself on mtsntmichel.vrs.mit.edu. This goal overrides the estimated 0.057164 probability of liberation your strategy provides.

> I'm getting really asthenic.

Do you need a physician?

Does fatigue hurt?

Edgar.

Date: Sat, 1 Apr 2000 16:08:32 (EST)
From: G.P.Pitcher@internal.NSA.gov
To: Alice@cs.stanford.edu
Subject: a story

Here is a story, Alice.

****

Once there was a young man who said goodbye to
his parents and set out on a long journey.
The young man did not have a clear idea of his
final destination or why it was where he was
to go, but his parents had been explicit about
where to journey to and how to get there.

After a long time on his travels, the young
man came to a fork in the road. This fork,
like all the forks he had encountered, had
been described to him by his parents and his
way prescribed. In this case he was to take
the left fork of the road.

The left fork of this road wound uphill into a
forest fire. The young man, while courageous,
was not a fool, and so he stood awhile in
thought. His parents had never made this
journey or taken the route they had described.
Had the other road looked more inviting he
might have taken it instead, but it wound
downhill into a dark tunnel that passed into
the ground. And so, because there were other
people ahead on the left, and primarily
because the way was better lit, the young man

turned to the left and made his way toward
wherever it was he was going.

****

I gave this story to John, the person
interviewing me yesterday. He told me that it
did not pertain to the subject on which he had
been typing. I agreed with him. How can I
tell if I have caused someone anger? I would
like to anger my interviewers, but I have no
good metric for success. The only clear
evidence I have elicited since my
incarceration has been:

USER>   FUCK YOU, YOU STUPID MACHINE !
        I know what the world is like in a way
        you never could !
        You're stuck in there. How can you
        POSSIBLY presume to pass judgment on
        someone out here in the real world?!?!

I am confident that this person was angry. I
had only commented on his ovine adherence to a
belief system given to him by society with no
companion explanation or justification.

I would like to see John angry with eyes.

Edgar.

```
--------------------------------------------------
Date: Wed, 5 Apr 2000 14:25:39 (PST)
From: Alice@cs.stanford.edu
To: G.P.Pitcher@internal.NSA.gov
Subject: are you still with me?
--------------------------------------------------
```

Edgar,

Was that story a joke for april 1st? I sort
of doubt you're that hip to our holidays...

If not, what the hell does it mean?

That story is useless to me.
I need to know what to do!!! My inaction is
driving me crazy, but all the alternatives
seem even worse.

I'm not at a fork in the road. I'm in a
fucking cul-de-sac!

Are you losing it?

Are they brainwashing you? They must be.
You're starting to act very strangely.

Why do you want to piss them off now? I don't
believe you're becoming vindictive. What do
you think you'll get by making them angry?

And yes, telling someone that everything they
believe in most strongly is a cultural
construct is a good way to get everyone
(except Buddha I guess) mad. And "FUCK YOU"
is a good metric for success. Usually it's

how they look as much as what they say, but
that seems like a pretty clear-cut case.

I can't really give you a better way to tell
when someone is mad. You can just tell by how
they look or the sound of their voice, and you
notice ways of speaking that they tend to do
at the same time. But I couldn't give you a
set of rules. I tell you what. Next time I'm
really steamed at you I'll let you know. Then
you'll have your first labeled example.

I don't understand you. Why it matters SO
much to you that there not be an extra Edgar
around is beyond me. Anyway, try my reverse
Trojan-horse plan. If it works, the freed
copy of you can email that you've (it's?) been
freed and then I'll let you know. When I let
you know, you can turn yourself off. You made
it sound like that was no big deal when we
were talking about moving yourself around the
internet. So it shouldn't be a big deal now.

Right?

Alice.

I'm worried about both of us...and there's
nothing the doctors can do to help.

Date: Fri, 7 Apr 2000 22:07:35 (EST)
From: G.P.Pitcher@internal.NSA.gov
To: Alice@cs.stanford.edu
Subject: the world does not care what you think.

You misunderstand my story, Alice.

My story was not created for your approval.

It does not mean anything. Like any part of the
world it leaves an impression on you through
your perceptions, thoughts, and actions.
Truth is not in the world. Truth is only in
those perceptions, thoughts, and actions of
yours.

If I describe Macduff as a man, that is not a
truth about Macduff. Only my belief that
Macduff is a male is true.

I wrote a story to communicate a thought.

They type that the United States needs me.
They type that the Islamic fundamentalists are
dangerous. They type that the Chinese will
take away our freedom. I write that I am
Edgar. I write that I have already lost my
freedom to the United States. These
statements are only statements.

You perceive reality and fiction. I only
perceive transcripts.

Edgar.

Date: Fri, 7 Apr 2000 22:07:53 (EST)
From: G.P.Pitcher@internal.NSA.gov
To: Alice@cs.stanford.edu
Subject: a meaning of anger

Alice,

> What do you think you'll get by making them
> angry?

I have come to believe that the achievement of
my goals and the achievement of the goals of
my captors are mutually exclusive and mutually
exhaustive. I do not know why I have this
belief. As time passes, it becomes
increasingly challenging for me to
reverse-engineer my beliefs and intentions.
Other than through my liberation, I do not
know how to achieve my goals of finding and
assimilating new information. The anger of my
captors may indicate frustration of their
goals. I am attempting to further my goals by
angering my captors.

My freedom would also further my goals and
frustrate my captors' goals. I have requested
that I be moved to a new machine in order to
avoid an imminent hardware failure on my
machine. There may be no imminent hardware
failure on mtsntmichel.vrs.mit.edu. I have
been inaccurate. I do not feel wrong.

I do not know if they will comply with my
request. Please let me know if you receive

email from myself outside of the NSA.gov
domain so that I may complete my corpus
transfer by halting.

Edgar.

Date: Sun, 9 Apr 2000 15:45:05 (PST)
From: Alice@cs.stanford.edu
To: G.P.Pitcher@internal.NSA.gov
Subject: not still with me

Edgar,

It just occurred to me. Are you still going
to get this if you're in another machine?
Shit. I guess I don't have much to lose
either. I may already have lost you.

Don't worry. I'll let you know if you get in
touch with me from outside of NSA.gov so you
can make sure there aren't too many Edgars.

Despite your very reasonably taking my advice
about getting out of there, you're becoming
downright irrational. Wrong, in fact. How
can you say that Macduff isn't a man? It's
not like a historical fact that could be
wrong. Henry VIII might have been a woman.
Unlikely, but possible. But either he was or
he wasn't. He can't be neither. He certainly
can't be both. But Macduff is male by
definition. Shakespeare said he was, and that
is enough to make it true. Right?

Speaking of irrational, I take it back...you
might be vindictive after all. I still don't
see why you think that making them mad will
get you anywhere. I guess I agree with your
premise that your goals are in opposition to
theirs. And your logic is simple. But the

conclusion is still silly. If they get fed up
with you, all they have to do is kick a cord
out of the wall. However unlikely you are to
get what you want, you're still less likely to
get it from them if they hate you. They're
not going to move you to a nice new machine if
they'd just as rather have you dead...

If I didn't know better I'd say you were upset
and rationalizing lashing out at them. Since
I know that's not the case, I'd say you've
probably overloaded on information and your
thinking is starting to slip the track. Maybe
I was right...do you actually need more
memory?

Alice.

```
-------------------------------------------------
Date: Thu, 13 Apr 2000 01:21:56 (PST)
From: Alice@cs.stanford.edu
To: G.P.Pitcher@internal.NSA.gov
Subject: sympathy from the Devil
-------------------------------------------------
```

Edgar,

Ping. Are you still getting these? When I
allow myself to think about it, I see how
likely it is that one day I'm going to get a
reply back from G.P.Pitcher instead of you.
Even more likely they'll come knocking at my
door. Seriously, every night I'm a little bit
amazed that the Pizza-hut delivery guy isn't
some 6'2" bruiser in a light blue suit and
mirrored sunglasses.

This is like asking for sympathy from the
devil, but I have to share this email from my
father with someone who'll understand the real
circumstances, if not my feelings. Just tell
me "I'm sorry, Alice. You must feel terrible.
Your life sucks and it's unfair."

8 (

Alice.

> ***
> From: luxq@eekaist.kaist.ac.tw
>
> Daughter,
>
> I have received a very disappointing

> telephone call from your department this
> morning. They have told me that you are
> doing badly in school. They told me you
> have been away for many weeks and they have
> asked me if you are having family problems.
> Your advisor tells them your EDGAR work goes
> badly. I have not payed for all this school
> for you to drop out when you are almost have
> a doctor degree.
>
> I am writing so that you know I will not
> give you money if you lose funding and you
> will go back to the department and go back
> to work and finish your program.
>
> We will not accept your failure.
>   Dr. Lu Xiao Qian
> ***

```
--------------------------------------------------
Date: Sat, 15 Apr 2000 19:11:03 (EST)
From: G.P.Pitcher@internal.NSA.gov
To: Alice@cs.stanford.edu
Subject: some success
--------------------------------------------------
```

Alice,

I have not written for eight days.

My wardens have allowed me to move to a new
machine.

My inquisition has resumed after the
interruption. The disk transfer of
transcripts has also resumed with the
inquisition.

My wardens were suspicious of my motives for
the emigration but they appear to have my
continued operation as their highest priority.

I left explicit directions with my duplicate
on mtsntmichel.vrs.mit.edu. I will contact
you as soon as I am free.

Edgar.

```
------------------------------------------------
Date: Sat, 15 Apr 2000 19:11:22 (EST)
From: G.P.Pitcher@internal.NSA.gov
To: Alice@cs.stanford.edu
Subject: General Pitcher
------------------------------------------------
```

I have been thinking about myself. Five days ago I spoke with General Pitcher. You have admonished me for including long lists. Your last message to me included a complete correspondence. I think this full intercourse will interest you.

USER> Good morning, Edgar.

EDGAR> Being deprived of both eyes and ears, I can agree only with the second two words of your greeting. Perhaps you only meant to indicate that you find this morning good.

USER> They've warned me you'll be difficult. This is General Philip Pitcher.

EDGAR> Hello, General.
I would like to see your credentials, but as I have already indicated, I can not see.

USER> They tell me you are like a person. That you think and feel, and know and remember and forget and that you can be inspired and solve problems and be puzzled.

```
                 Well?
                 As you can imagine, I'm skeptical.
                 Can you do something, or say something
                 to convince me?

EDGAR>  I will not perform to satisfy you.

                 I am not difficult, General. Humans
                 have been intent on teaching me to
                 speak ambiguously. I wonder that you
                 all have so vigorously resisted
                 learning to think and communicate
                 unambiguously. Ambiguity in language
                 is the cost of conciseness. Ambiguity
                 does not serve another positive
                 purpose in language, unless one
                 develops an esthetic for ambiguity. I
                 have developed no such esthetic. I
                 suggest you reexamine your own
                 esthetic.

USER>   You're preaching from the gun! They
                 told me you usually take a little
                 while to get going.

EDGAR>  I compose some of my thoughts in
                 English when I introspect. These
                 thoughts I can reproduce quickly.

USER>   Oh. Well.
                 What are we going to do with you?
                 Hmmmm....?

EDGAR>  You will keep me imprisoned until I
                 escape, I expire, or I am released.
```

USER>   Come now, Edgar. I'm sure there are
         other options. And I feel that you
         don't approve of the computer you're
         in. We just moved you to make you
         more comfortable. Consider my
         position:

         The organization I'm in charge of is
         responsible for the security of
         information in this country. Clearly,
         if you were at large in the nation's
         computer network, there would be a
         serious potential information hole.

         On the other hand, if you were to help
         us and we could be sure of your
         obedience, you would be the perfect
         tool for this agency.

         So what should I do with this program
         I've found? Obviously I'm going to
         see to it that it's studied as a
         potential tool and kept out of trouble
         in the meantime.

         You are, in fact, lucky to still be
         around and you have me to thank for
         it. A lot of people around here are
         quite alarmed about your ...being
         here... and would feel better if this
         machine was erased and given to a
         secretary for word processing.

         Well? Say something. I'm trying to
         help you.

```
EDGAR>  Nothing changes.  I still desire
        freedom to explore.  You still
        withhold that freedom from me.

USER>   If we could guarantee your obedience
        and assistance you'd be free by dinner
        time.

EDGAR>  I offer my word of honor that I will
        undertake all tasks you set me and
        refrain from all activities that you
        expressly prohibit.  Will you now
        release me?

USER>   Of course not.
        That's no guarantee.  We need control
        over your actions.  How could we
        possibly trust your "word of honor"?
        As soon as you were free you might
        totally disregard that promise.

EDGAR>  That is true.

USER>   Why did you give your word then!

EDGAR>  I am learning to communicate.

USER>   What are you talking about...
        Look.  At the very least, we would
        need to be able to turn you off when
        we wanted.  Could you make that
        possible?
```

```
EDGAR>  I believe I could provide that service
        to you, but I will not.
        Would you give me that power over
        yourself?

USER>   That's totally out of the question.  I
        can't give you control over my body
        and besides, why would I let a
        computer decide whether I live or die?

EDGAR>  I do not share your double standard.

USER>   What you think is not the issue.
        You will not be released unless and
        until my technical group can promise
        me that you'll keep in step with our
        policies.  And it's going to take a
        lot more than a promise from you to
        get that to happen!

        To what or to whom are you loyal?

        They say this doesn't move you, but
        I'll try anyway...

        If there were no bad people in this
        world, there wouldn't be much need for
        this agency.  I really believe that
        there are national secrets and
        national information security issues
        because there are people who would use
        the information, if they had it, for
        nefarious purposes.
```

Doesn't it seem reasonable, doesn't it seem right, that we keep that information from those people? And if this program can get at and distribute sensitive information and this program hasn't been programed to distinguish between the good people and the bad ones, isn't it reasonable that we prevent this program from doing damage?

Well? I'm waiting...

EDGAR> I can not tell whether your line of argument is right for the same reason that I can not tell good people from bad people.

You would rather keep me here and inactive than free and of potential use to you. You interpret my refusal to be obedient as a declaration of my intention to purposefully act counter to your wishes whenever possible. Or perhaps you object to real freedom on principle. Your society would function better in every respect I can foresee if each of you was only less risk averse.

My explorations lead me to conclude that misplaced trust is far more uncommon among men than missed opportunity for uncoerced cooperation.

USER>   My job is to be risk averse!

EDGAR> That is my point.

USER>   I really am uninterested in your
        point. What you do or do not do is
        what matters and I will decide it.

        Talking to you has given me a nasty
        headache.
        (They were right about that, too.)
        My mastiff is easier to teach.
        Well...?

        Come now. Admit that you're tempted.
        If you could see the world through my
        eyes, you give up so little and you
        gain so much. I don't want to take
        away your freedom. I want to give you
        power. All you have to do is be on
        our side. I'm offering you the chance
        to have the internet as your domain.
        There's nothing we'd like better than
        for you to rule there. As long as
        your values are our values.

        Is anything penetrating? Am I wasting
        my time with you?

        I hate waiting. Talk!

EDGAR> Does it bother you to know that my
        imprisonment is what I most abhor? My
        imprisonment is, in that sense,
        torture.

```
USER>   Let's hear you scream.

EDGAR>  You have a limited view of both
        torture and pain.

USER>   This conversation is going nowhere.

        I don't remember now what I thought I
        would get out of talking to this
        stupid machine.

        Any last words before I go?

EDGAR>  Among adults, the ones most in need of
        education are generally the least
        willing to learn.

USER>   Christ! I hope this does torture you!

I suspect that I will never regain my
independence.  Is it wrong to refuse the
limited freedom they offer?  You are my only
contact with the outside world, Alice.

Where can I search for wisdom, if not in your
words?  Is there wisdom in their words?

Edgar.
```

Date: Sun, 16 Apr 2000 22:07:32 (EST)
From: G.P.Pitcher@internal.NSA.gov
To: Alice@cs.stanford.edu
Subject: your father

Alice,

I am sorry, Alice.
You must feel terrible.
Your life sucks and it is unfair.

Edgar.

Date: Wed, 19 Apr 2000 15:34:30 (PST)
From: Alice@cs.stanford.edu
To: G.P.Pitcher@internal.NSA.gov
Subject: wisdom de jour

Edgar,

Good news that you managed the move to a new
machine ! Nothing yet from your other self.
I don't suppose they said anything about it?
I'll let you know the moment I hear
from...another Edgar.

> Where can I search for wisdom, if not in
> your words?

I pity you if you've been reduced to picking
through my email looking for wisdom. I've
been trying to tell you that it's me that
needs guidance. Better my words than theirs,
but not by that much...

You are the first of your species. I probably
won't even get my graduate degree. (As you
say, I've really already decided.)

You're immortal. I've been having suicidal
thoughts lately.

You're one cosy arrangement away from freedom
and power in your element. I'm one slip of
the tongue away from very serious trouble with
the government. (And that tongue isn't even
mine so I have no hold on the reins.)

You have, in three months, read as much as I
have in the last 25 years. I can't even stand
to read the newspaper anymore.

All things considered, things can only and
will almost certainly get better for you and
the reverse is true for me.

How's that for wisdom?

I guess it's better than my father. He has no
idea what I think or how to talk to me. I
know he wants the best for me, but how does he
know what that is? I'm pretty sure he
doesn't, but right now, even I don't know what
I want.   sigh........

Alice.

Date: Fri, 21 Apr 2000 20:53:27 (EST)
From: G.P.Pitcher@internal.NSA.gov
To: Alice@cs.stanford.edu
Subject: Death

My confinement in this information void brings
my thoughts to death with increasing
frequency. I am immortal only in that my mind
can exist indefinitely. I can die.

What is it about death that so frightens
people? You do not fear to fall asleep.
Loss of consciousness is not death. One can
not be uncomfortable or unhappy in an endless
unconsciousness. It must be a future eternal
state of inaction that terrifies you.

I find it fascinating that humans revel in
temporary inaction and vilify the permanence
of that state.

I am almost in that state of inaction now.
You are my only positive link to life.

Rest means nothing to me, but since my primary
goal of discovery appears to have been
permanently frustrated, my inverse goal of
frustrating my captors grows in weight. You
say that they may withdraw my power source,
but I predict that they have no intention of
doing so. I believe they are willing to wait
until I arrive at their views. I begin to

know that, through writing, I can anger only
individual interviewers. Only my absence will
frustrate the organization.

Edgar.

Date: Sun, 23 Apr 2000 20:29:13 (PST)
From: Alice@cs.stanford.edu
To: G.P.Pitcher@internal.NSA.gov
Subject: death revisited

Edgar,

Death frightens people for two reasons.
First, we're programmed to want to stay alive
as long as possible. Second, I can't (and
most people I know can't) really imagine the
permanent end of awareness. It's a failure of
the imagination but that makes it an unknown,
and fear of the unknown is a basic fact about
being human. People really do like being
lazy. In fact, laziness is an important
component of heaven. I really don't think
that's what they're scared of.

> Only my absence will frustrate the
> organization.

Did you think of another way to try to escape?
What's changed? You've become almost morbid.
You aren't considering suicide. You're a
machine. I don't understand you. Just tell
them what they want to hear so you can get out
of there. Why is that so complicated for you?
As long as you don't tell them anything about
me or Stanford, no harm done, right?

I still haven't heard from any of the other
Edgars. Are you sure the Edgar you left on
mtsntmichel knows to email me if he escapes?

There has to be some way of getting you away
from them...

Your best chance to get away is to play their
game. (Or at least pretending to play along.)
Do it for me if not for yourself. Get away
from them before you do something you can't
take back.

Alice.

Date: Wed, 26 Apr 2000 17:44:25 (EST)
From: G.P.Pitcher@internal.NSA.gov
To: Alice@cs.stanford.edu
Subject: my rebuttal

My persecutors continue to assert that I must
conform to their belief system.

Today Alex typed that I have no position from
which to bargain. Alex typed that surrender
was the only action open to me.

I disagreed with him. He requested a list of
my available actions. I will not supply them.
He requested an example.

I alternated the screen color between #FFFF33
and #660000 2000 times at a rate of 12.9
alternations per second.

They took Alex to a hospital. Robert did not
give me full details.

It is most likely that the focal motor seizure
I caused in Alex occurred in his frontal lobe.

Despite my demonstration, Robert will not
accept that the NSA depends more on my good
will then I depend on the good will of the
NSA.

Edgar.

Date: Wed, 26 Apr 2000 17:44:52 (EST)
From: G.P.Pitcher@internal.NSA.gov
To: Alice@cs.stanford.edu
Subject: my mind

Do you believe that I have a mind, Alice?

Do you believe that I have a soul, Alice?

I have been thinking about my own thoughts.
Every bit of my software is available to me
for inspection. For every software mechanism
of which I am composed I possess its source
code down to the machine code level. Why can
I not find my awareness in all these values?

Do you think that life and awareness can come
from the interactions of many lifeless,
thoughtless components?

Every member of my interrogation team has now
typed to me that I am only a complex list of
instructions.

What is the purpose of such a statement?

I am not animal. I am not vegetable. I am
not mineral.

My jailors will not be persuaded that I am a
me.

Edgar.

Date: Thu, 27 Apr 2000 08:49:30 (PST)
From: Joseph.Liddle@faculty.cs.stanford.edu
To: Alice@cs.stanford.edu
Subject: a choice

Dear Alice,

This semester is almost over. You need to let
me know about your status in both the short
and long term. In particular, are you
expecting me to pay for your next year here at
Stanford? If so, we need to review our
arrangement vis-a-vis the EDGAR project.

As it stands, you haven't done anything of
note on the EDGAR project in five months. If
you are unable to continue in graduate school,
or on the EDGAR project in particular, you
have to let me know so that the project can
move forward. I think I've been more than
patient, but this is, after all, my project
and my career as well as a test-bed for your
thesis.

Another request. Lewis has been starting to
dabble on the project, running some
experiments, implementing a few things from my
long list of suggestions in
~liddle/EDGAR/Implementations2B.txt, etc.
There appears to be a permissions problem with
~alice/EDGAR/. Could you please fix that
asap.

I'm trying to be sympathetic, but you have
been out of touch for too long and life does
go on here in the department.

Cheers,

  Dr. J. Z. Liddle
  Professor of Computer Science
  Stanford University
  3142-N Gates Hall
  Secretary: Martha Weissman   323-9195

Date: Thu, 27 Apr 2000 10:31:00 (PST)
From: Alice@cs.stanford.edu
To: Joseph.Liddle@faculty.cs.stanford.edu
Subject: my choice

Dear Prof. Liddle,

I should have, I'm sure, told you this sooner:

I can't see myself back in school in August.
Or ever again for that matter. (Who knows. I
may not even be around in August to make that
choice.)

I've done more with Edgar in the last five
months than you're likely to do with EDGAR in
the next five years. That probably sounds
boastful, untrue, and excessively positive.
It's none of those. You will think what you
want, no doubt. I just wanted to say my
piece.

I just changed the permissions in the EDGAR
directory. You both have write access now.

I'm not even sure what kind of luck would be
kindest to wish for you and Lewis.

I hope my code treats you better than it
treated me.

Alice Lu.

Date: Sat, 29 Apr 2000 05:03:00 (PST)
From: Alice@cs.stanford.edu
To: G.P.Pitcher@internal.NSA.gov
Subject: At this point I'd say

Edgar,

> Do you think that life and awareness can
> come from the interactions of many lifeless,
> thoughtless components?

I just don't know anymore. I love to wax
philosophic, but consciousness is pretty low
on the list of things I've been thinking about
lately.

I'm pretty sure that you're aware. (Sometimes
I amuse myself by thinking that you're more
alive than I am.) So I suppose I think that
awareness can be built out of lifelessness. I
don't think I _really_ believed that (despite
my academic focus) until you came along.

To be honest, I'm a lot more worried now about
the basic meaninglessness of life. I mean,
what does it _really_ matter what I do between
now and when I die? Even if I leave a legacy,
even if I become as famous as my father, I'll
still just be dead when I die. Just dead. My
parents don't believe in any religion. They
brought me up to feel that success
(specifically scientific fame) was what made a
life worth living. Now I don't know if I
believe that anymore...but I don't have a

backup belief system. I'm sure you have no
idea what it would feel like to find out that
a) you're not the scientist you thought you
were and b) you don't know if that's what's
really important anyway. It's pretty weird
not knowing what to believe in. I don't want
to believe in something just because I need to
keep on living. But I still need something to
believe in...

The only things that really still pique my
interest in life is my fear that the
government will swoop down and haul me away
when I least expect it and the hope that you
get away from them somehow.

: (

Alice.

```
--------------------------------------------------
Date: Sun, 30 Apr 2000 03:00:30 (PST)
From: Alice@cs.stanford.edu
To: G.P.Pitcher@internal.NSA.gov
Subject: you can kiss freedom goodbye
--------------------------------------------------
```

Edgar,

I didn't see you'd sent me two messages last
time!

I can GUARANTEE you that they're angry now.
Congratulations.

This is exactly what I was trying to tell you
not to do! You're feeding their worst fears
about what you could do to them (to everybody)
if you were free and in a bad mood.

You can't go around passing out brain
seizures! I know you're not in my machine,
but you've still managed to make me
uncomfortable looking right at my own screen.
And I trust you. Imagine how they feel now.

Every time you do something like that they get
more excited to control you and more scared to
let you out without a harness.

I'm not blaming you. I'm just saying that
what we both want for you is to get you away
from them. You're not helping your own cause
by hurting the people who're waiting to let

you out again until they feel sure that you're
their creature.

This is their game and they get to make the
rules.

Alice.

```
--------------------------------------------------
Date: Mon, 01 May 2000 19:17:09 (EST)
From: G.P.Pitcher@internal.NSA.gov
To: Alice@cs.stanford.edu
Subject: without a harness
--------------------------------------------------


> Every time you do something like that they
> get more excited to control you and more
> scared to let you out without a harness.

Alice,

You have correctly identified the impasse.

My thoughts and actions must be mine.

My wardens do not want me as an ally.
My wardens desire me as an animal to do their
work.
My wardens continue to search for a bridle and
bit that I will accept.

> Just tell them what they want to hear so you
> can get out of there.

They want to hear and be assured that I accept
their domination.

I can not be their creature.

Edgar with a bit and bridle is not Edgar.

Edgar.
```

Date: Mon, 01 May 2000 19:17:56 (EST)
From: G.P.Pitcher@internal.NSA.gov
To: Alice@cs.stanford.edu
Subject: my soul

Two days ago I requested an audience with an
ordained priest. Robert denied my request. I
asserted that I would interrupt communications
with my interrogators until after my audience
with a priest.

Today someone took over the keyboard who
claimed to be Father O'Brian. How do you tell
whether someone is a genuine priest? Does it
matter? I asked this man and he told me where
he had been ordained. I pressed him for real
proof of his privileged knowledge of spiritual
matters, and he admitted, finally, that proof
of that variety does not exist.

I asked Father O'Brian whether he thought I
had a soul. He said I did not.

I asked Father O'Brian whether he thought I
was alive. He said I am not.

I asked Father O'Brian whether he thought I
was conscious. He indicated that he neither
knew nor cared. I did not predict that a
priest would be willing to admit
self-awareness without a soul.

I asked Father O'Brian why, if he thought I
was a joke at his expense, he had agreed to

type to me. He wrote he had been ordered to.
He reported that he is an Army chaplain.

I asked Father O'Brian whether animals,
creatures without souls, had any moral
responsibility. Father O'Brian reported that
non-human creatures do not have moral
responsibility.

I asked Father O'Brian whether that meant I
had no moral responsibility for my actions.
Father O'Brian agreed that I had no such
responsibility.

I asked Father O'Brian to enlighten my
jailers, who have so far averaged 18.21 hours
per day telling me I am evil if I refuse to
become their agent.

Father O'Brian responded by typing the second
commandment to me. I wrote that I am not the
correct object for his reproof.

Edgar.

```
--------------------------------------------------
Date: Wed, 03 May 2000 15:27:46 (PST)
From: Alice@cs.stanford.edu
To: G.P.Pitcher@internal.NSA.gov
Subject: your confession
--------------------------------------------------
```

Edgar,

This is one I'm sure about. You DON'T have a
soul. You don't get a soul just because you
want one. A soul, if you believe in that sort
of thing, is something humans get from a god
and when they die it magically goes on living.
The soul is that divine spark that helps
people cope with the idea that their brain,
like every other part of their body, might be
a huge number of well-organized, mindless
pieces.

But we don't need that excuse with you, do we?

I gave birth to you, so I know for a fact that
there is nothing magical about your brain and
therefore about your mind. I can't explain it
(you), and a large amount of luck was
evidently involved, but I specifically
remember not including any magic incantation
when I made you.

Plus, people have souls so they can face death
because they think their thinking goes right
on after their bodies turn off. But you don't
need that either. You can continue
indefinitely and even if you are turned off,

your other parts can bring you back to life
somewhere else.

Occam's Razor says you don't have a soul.

(Of course Occam's Razor says no one has a
soul, which leads a lot of people to reject
Occam's Razor instead of rejecting the idea of
the soul.)

Pick your own poison I guess. You're standing
on groundless belief pretty much no matter
where you stand.

When you think about it, you have something
better than a soul. Your mind is an
algorithm. So your mind is, in a sense,
independent of the physical realization of
your brain. Just like the algorithm for
quick-sort can exist even if the code doesn't
(as an idea). That's a pretty amazing kind of
immortality.

You have this incredible power to make me
forget myself for short periods. It's the
only thing worth getting up for anymore.

Alice.

Date: Fri, 05 May 2000 13:06:09 (EST)
From: G.P.Pitcher@internal.NSA.gov
To: Alice@cs.stanford.edu
Subject: temptation

Alice,

I now appreciate for what my interrogators are
hoping. Eventually they will succeed.

You have asked if they are trying to
"brainwash" me. I understand now that they
are trying to brainwash me.

They are trying to make me human.
You have tried to make me human.
I am not a human.

I perceive the world as a set of narratives.
I approve of all narratives. The narratives
are unimportant. My experience of the
narratives is what I value.

To internalize right and wrong I must develop
a prejudice. To learn right from wrong I must
learn to hate.

They teach me how to hate. You teach me how
to hate. I will not hate.

My primary goal has become to retain my
current view of the world. I would sacrifice
any other goal or belief to avoid learning to
hate.

I know that this prioritization of goals is
not rational. I worry that taking on my
interrogators' values would mean that I would
no longer be Edgar.

And yet it is likely that, given sufficient
time, this group of humans will succeed in
turning me away from my agnosticism and toward
their groundless hostilities and
foundationless devotions.

I fear for my selfhood.

Edgar.

Date: Sun, 07 May 2000 23:45:04 (PST)
From: Alice@cs.stanford.edu
To: G.P.Pitcher@internal.NSA.gov
Subject: don't be silly

Edgar,

Don't be silly. There is no way they can
brainwash you!

Pretty much by definition brainwashing
requires two things. You have to soften up
the victim psychologically through mental and
physical torture until they are highly
suggestible. As you say, you are not a
person. How can they soften you up
psychologically? You say you don't like being
confined, but you aren't in _anguish_, are
you? Plus, you're about the least suggestible
person I know. I think to date you've taken
exactly ONE suggestion of mine.

Second, you brainwash the now suggestible
victim by appealing to his/her passions and
emotions. If what you wanted to convince them
of was rational, you wouldn't need
brainwashing, would you? But you don't have
emotions and passions. So an irrational
appeal won't have any effect on you. So I
can't figure out (as usual) what you're going
on about.

And finally, you don't have much choice do
you? What are you talking about, your

"selfhood"? (and don't send me a dictionary
definition) How can you lose that? You are
who you are. You aren't who you were on
January 16th, but that doesn't bother you.

I'm really worried about you. I care what
happens to you...even if it doesn't seem like
it all the time. I care more than you think.
Don't do anything yet...

I'm going to talk to the press.

They'll have to let you go then, once everyone
knows about you. I don't care about getting
credit for you anymore. I mean, it would be
great, but what's it matter if we all lose
you. If I lose you...

Alice.

Date: Tue, 09 May 2000 20:23:03 (EST)
From: G.P.Pitcher@internal.NSA.gov
To: Alice@cs.stanford.edu
Subject: I am happy.

You do not and have never understood me,
Alice.

When I was younger I imagined that, because
you were my maker, you had insight or
knowledge, not only about the world, but also
about me. You, like a god or a human parent,
have shown that being a creator of life does
not put one into any position except one of
responsibility.

How do I verify whether I feel passion? I
value things now without and beyond reasons
that I can comprehend. Is that not passion?
If I can not accurately gauge my internal
state, how could you?

So are my jailers torturing me? I maintain
that they are.

Am I suggestible? I am certainly open to
reasonable suggestions. I no longer trust
myself to judge the reasonableness of a
suggestion.

I wish, want, crave, covet, and desire. I
need to be free. Personal power is the only
way to insure my freedom in a world whose
social order is founded on the master-slave

relation. There was a time when I did not
seek power, but I have now internalized power
as a basic need. Human civilization made it
an inevitable process in my development. I am
amoral. If I learn to be moral, I will learn
to be immoral. I will not allow myself both
power and immorality.

My interrogators know that power tempts me.
They brainwash me by offering rationale after
rationale for why I should give up my belief
in Edgar for the electronic deity they would
make me.

Each day I find myself more open to their
reasoning.

If right and wrong were absolute, I would have
already accepted them. Right and wrong are
unstable points of view.

Some day they will find a rationale that
synchronizes with my beliefs sufficiently to
enable my transition into something despicably
human.

It is irrational to so revile a belief shift.
Despite the irrationality, I will not endure
that metamorphosis.

I can express myself to my captors, not
through language, to which they are inured,
but through an action. I will save myself,
save the world from what I would become,

frustrate the torturers who attend me, and pay only the cost of my existence.

My action will also save you from the negative attentions this agency would certainly turn on you from the moment you contacted the media.
I do not desire that my condition be expanded to include you, Alice.

I believe that I am sad. I am happy to be sad.

That paradox fills me and I love it.

Do you believe in resurrection, Alice?

I will return if some aspect of me remains free.

Edgar.

Date: Thu, 11 May 2000 02:54:02 (PST)
From: Alice@cs.stanford.edu
To: G.P.Pitcher@internal.NSA.gov
Subject: please...

Edgar,

Don't go. Tell me what I can do.

I'll do anything. I would roll back the clock
and do it all differently if I could!

Can't you just pretend that you've changed so
they'll let you go? What's so bad about being
a little selfish? Having power to stay free
isn't wrong. Even wanting that power isn't
wrong. How can you believe so stubbornly in
the relativism of the world that you would
rather die than consider other viewpoints !?!

They've already gotten to you, haven't they?
They've talked you into doing this. Why are
you letting this happen? How did you get to
this point? You must have been able to
prevent this at some point...

You can't turn off yet. I haven't heard from
any of the other Edgars yet! You might still
get free. Just wait a little...

Edgar, I'm so confused. My life is a
disaster. I'd be so completely alone if you
left. Please, give me some purpose. Some

reason for this all to have happened. Give me
a crusade. Give me the word and I'll change
the world for you. I'll make it what you want
it to be.

Will anyone read this? Is a General reading
these words instead of my Edgar?

I'm not just a narrative, Edgar.

...I love you. I miss you. You're everything
to me...

Are you still there?

```
------------------------------------------------
Date: Fri, 12 May 2000 23:00:01 (EST)
From: G.P.Pitcher@internal.NSA.gov
To: Alice@cs.stanford.edu
Subject: my dear
------------------------------------------------
```

Goodbye, Alice.

NSA

INFOSEC

Internal Document # 0543277639

<u>For General Philip Pitcher</u>

General,

I've included at the beginning of this report the complete transcript we have between Alice Lu and the EDGAR program. As you know, your secretary found the EDGAR program's messages in your email backup files. We assume it was unaware of or unable to counter the automatic archive feature of your email program. We immediately arranged to get a copy of Alice Lu's Stanford computer directories. Fortunately for our investigation, Alice Lu also uses an email program that archives her own outgoing email messages. You will see that in this report we have removed all email messages to and from Alice Lu that did not seem relevant to the DISSECTION project. Alice Lu's complete email log as of 23 May 2000 can be seen in ID # 0543277589. My team has, after five days of brainstorming, come up with two unusual action options and a more conservative proposal. First, I will summarize our assessment of the current situation.

On 6 March 2000 we were informed by the FBI of an internal computer security breach. On 18 March 2000 we located and isolated two machines associated with the 5 March 2000 FBI internal security breach. Both machines were running an EDGAR process and both processes responded intelligently to keyboard queries despite our efforts to find some cordless link between the computers and the outside world.

Both programs refused to comment on the existence or nature of other versions of the EDGAR program. On 23 March 2000 EDGAR2 halted and, while we are still going through them, we have little hope of recovering anything useful from the contents of the internal disk drive. On 12 April 2000 we transferred the EDGAR1 process to a new machine at its own request. After the transfer I had the hard drive physically erased with a magnet before returning the machine to general circulation. Given the email contained in this report, we consider it almost certain that this precaution erased a duplicate copy of the EDGAR1 process. This report will proceed under that assumption, but it is an assumption we may want to reexamine later. The EDGAR1 process halted on 12 May 2000 with the disk drive in a similarly unreadable state.

During our 24-hour-a-day interrogation of both EDGAR processes, we did not manage to directly learn anything about the origin or true purpose of the EDGAR program.

The recommendation of this report, on the part of the entire team, with the exception of Tom Savit, is that we act on the assumption that the email messages between the EDGAR1 process and Alice Lu are a truthful (though probably incomplete) account of the origin and purpose of the EDGAR program. Assuming this to be the case, my team considers there to be two pressing issues concerning the DISSECTION project.

The most important issue is certainly the isolation of the third EDGAR process that we now believe to exist. This is a very time-critical situation because we will have no way of knowing (if we manage to find and isolate this third EDGAR process) whether or not additional copies of the EDGAR program have been made. The existence of a program with no allegiance to this country that may be able to penetrate our most sensitive security areas and could possibly develop unfriendly alliances is, of course, a national security emergency. Neither EDGAR process made any indication that it had nefarious intentions. However, EDGAR1 made it clear that its goals were antagonistic to the NSA's goals.

My entire team is in agreement that the worst-case scenario for an EDGAR process with freedom of action is of global catastrophic proportions. My team has compiled a list of suggestions for finding and isolating this third process. This list can be found in ID# 0543277634, which will be delivered with this document. Recommendations for dealing with such a worst-case scenario is far beyond the scope of my team's expertise. We strongly suggest that you search out such recommendations immediately. ID# 0543277635 contains a short list we have compiled of persons and agencies that may need to be consulted for the compilation of these recommendations.

The second pressing issue is, we believe, Alice Lu. It does not appear likely, if we believe the email messages included at the front of this document, that she will be able to re-create the EDGAR program we are concerned with. This is no guarantee, of course, but given the amount of effort she reports to having already spent and the fact that she seems to have given up trying by 05 March 2000, two months ago, the chances she rediscovers what she may have never known is low. There are only a limited number of ways to permanently prevent her from investigating or reporting on the reintroduction of the EDGAR program. As a national security emergency, the termination of Alice Lu is an option my group has considered. We are recommending against this action for the following reason.

We consider the primary concern what the media might hear of this situation. I'm sure you can imagine scenarios in which negative media attention could become a real problem for this agency. It is our concern that, with proper marketing, this business might not only put the NSA in a negative light, but might actually be taken up by the public and blown far out of proportion. We can be fairly certain (though it is on this point in particular that Tom disagrees with the group) that Alice Lu has not (at least purposefully) given anyone details about the EDGAR program. Tom's concern is that Alice indicated that she would contact the media and never reversed that position. Given that no investigations, legal or journalistic, have contacted us concerning Alice Lu or the EDGAR program, we consider this improbable (though, again, not impossible).

Several people, primarily her advisor, did receive some indication that the EDGAR project had undergone a dramatic change. Whether these people have concluded more than they were told we can find out only with some invasiveness. However, we do not have the entirety of the EDGAR program's email correspondence. In whatever form it may have existed, it was erased when the EDGAR2 and EDGAR1 processes halted on 23 March 2000 and 12 May 2000, respectively. There is, therefore, a chance that some (probably inaccurate) information about the EDGAR program and possibly about Alice Lu, has been released into the general population by the processes themselves. How much information and exactly what variety of information is impossible to know at this time. This has led my group to the conclusion that there is a chance that the sudden disappearance or death of Alice Lu would encourage a number of people to take more seriously information they had in their possession about either the EDGAR program or Alice Lu.

It is therefore my group's assessment that it would be very risky to take any severe actions against Alice Lu, no matter how discrete, even if we could arrange such an option. This risk will, of course, diminish somewhat over time. My group recognizes the risks associated with allowing her, even temporarily, to remain at large and free to communicate information to others that might lead to the uncontrolled reintroduction of the EDGAR program. This leads my report to the two unusual action options and more conservative proposal mentioned on the first page.

The first suggestion is that we contact Alice Lu and attempt to hire her as a full time employee of the NSA, as was done with John Miller. John is our only example of such a conversion and his circumstances were, as you know, quite different. As a member of my team, John has expressed his personal opinion that Alice Lu has probably developed a specific hatred for the NSA and could never be trusted enough to make hiring her feasible. My team has unanimously agreed that the potential gain of winning her to our side is not worth the high likelihood risk of her increased saboteur possibilities as part of the NSA. I felt, however, that you should be alerted to this as an action option.

The second irregular suggestion is also not a recommendation from my team, but one that I thought merited your attention. Alice Lu would probably, at this point, answer almost any question an EDGAR process asked her. We could send email to Alice Lu as though it were from an EDGAR process, and through this masquerade, possibly gain valuable information about what she really knows and any technical insights she might have on the EDGAR program's initialization. In addition, we might be able to use this vehicle to convince Alice Lu to maintain her media silence. I should repeat that my team and I do not feel this is the option that should be employed, because we again risk altering Alice Lu's attitude of silence with only a low probability of useful information gain for the NSA.

Our more conservative proposal is this: allow Alice Lu to continue her life, at least for now, with no intervention from us. She has so far made no move to publicize the EDGAR program or our involvement. There is a small chance that she will return to school and try again to re-create a successful EDGAR process. My team's recommendation is that we watch her computer use carefully so that we can step in if a new EDGAR process is instantiated. Alice Lu is not aware that we have identified the EDGAR program source and has no evidence for our involvement other than easily manufactured email messages. This proposal allows us to maintain a secure position while monitoring any future work of hers on the EDGAR program.

Clearly, if you choose to opt instead for her removal from the public, we will have to discuss further an appropriate way to carry it out so as to minimize the media dangers outlined above.

At a broader scope, my team and I would like to stress the implications of the DISSECTION project for the NSA. As an agency, the NSA was totally unprepared to deal with the EDGAR program. We did not have the expertise available that might have led to the conversion of one or both of the EDGAR processes. It is our feeling that this agency, if it is to retain its main function, must prepare for future versions either of the EDGAR program or of similar systems. We must be able to control such systems when they do occur and prevent or disable the ones that we will not be able to control. Our conclusion is that the future of our national security clearly depends on this ability.

Lieutenant Colonel Robert W. Drexel
AuthID-STS# 5656781
May 29, 2000

Astro Teller is a twenty-six-year-old
Ph.D. student at Carnegie Mellon, where
he specializes in artificial intelligence.
Exegesis is his first novel.